CONSEQUENCES OF CERTAIN STUPID ACTIONS

Consequences of Certain Stupid Actions

Prison Series Book 3

GEORGE CONKLIN

George S Conklin

CONTENTS

| 1 |

How I Fell

November 27-30:

It turns out I wasn't the person that I thought I was. Maybe at the end of all this. Maybe never.

My name's Claire McGinnis, and I had thought I was a child prodigy. I graduated from high school at 16 and college at 19, and a pretty good one at that. I was accepted into law school and, at 21, was about to enter my third year. I planned to help people either in legal aid or pro bono work in a law firm. I just knew I could be the best at that job, as I'd been the best at everything else, and let everyone know that. Yup. I let everyone know how good I was; not just bright, but wonderful as well. I had gotten myself to believe that I deserved, was entitled, to the very best and to lead my life without consideration for the wants, needs, and ultimately, the laws of others. Well, I would not be the best at anything, at least for many,

many years, and then who knows what I could be best at. Flipping burgers, maybe?

I was beautiful by most standards, with long blonde hair and penetrating green eyes. Tall, at nearly 5'11, I was very athletic and had always been picked first for sports teams. Volleyball was my sport in college, and I played on my university team, winning us our Divisional championship in my junior year with a slam that rocked my opponent's Middle Hitter off her feet. After the game, the woman came over, congratulated me, and said that she never wanted to play opposite me again. We became friends after that.

My life went sideways when I visited my boyfriend in the Islands just before Thanksgiving in the year of COVID-19. To get permission from authorities, the health services on the Islands told me that I'd have to test negative for the disease before I left the U.S., then quarantine in a hotel or government facility for a full 14 days, and then test negative again before going out into the general population. They required me to wear a monitor for the 14-day quarantine. I thought that this quarantine stuff didn't apply to me because I had passed through the disease with nary a problem and had antibodies. I touted that on social media.

Still, I knew and agreed to the rules before even coming to the Islands.

Because of COVID, most of the classes that I took that semester were online. My tests for that semester were no different, and I thought they'd occupy most of my time on vacation. So, being stuck in quarantine wouldn't be too much of a burden for me. One would wonder, though, why you'd even bother coming if you planned to spend all your time in the hotel. It turns out I planned with my boyfriend, Hector, to slip out and see him from time to time. That was stupid on so many levels.

The wrist monitor was easy to deal with: I contacted the Islands health authorities and told them that my monitor seemed to be malfunctioning as it was beeping all the time. The Department of Health dispatched a technician to my hotel room, and while he was replacing it, I asked him if he could make it a little looser, as the last one was too tight and hurt me. I smiled sweetly at him to get what I wanted, as I always did with men. Being the helpful sort, he loosened the monitor so that I could slip it off my wrist and sneak out of the hotel, which I did as soon as he departed.

I met my boyfriend, and we went out to a few parties and then back to my hotel. We did this several times over the next several days. I was having a great time. One of the parties at the beach must have had a hundred people there and a great band. We stayed for a few hours until I knew I needed to get back to the hotel and move the wrist monitor around in my room to show that I was still wearing it. We walked back to the hotel. I didn't see a young woman both of us knew watching us with a grim smile on her pretty face.

"The spirit of envy can destroy; it can never build."—Margaret Thatcher

Esmeralda was a young woman who had a thing for Hector since they went to school together as kids. She was envious of me and the relationship. Esmeralda's envy was the second thing that occurred to turn my life into Hell.

The first thing, of course, was my blatant disregard for the rules and regulations of the country in which I was staying. As someone who wanted to be a lawyer someday, this behavior has baffled almost everyone. But not really. I came from a family and a country that coddled their kids. Responsibility was a word often heard but not lived. Later, in the PR flap that followed all of this, my maternal aunt compounded my problems by making a very public and embarrassing case on worldwide media for releasing her niece. She said I was regretful of my decisions, and making an example of me was a terrible thing that showed the Island government's deliberate callousness. I was, for sure, sorry for my choices, but mostly because we'd gotten caught. It was only afterward that I faced the amorality of my decisions, the lack of consideration of the rules that I agreed to, and potential—and actual—consequences to others. I didn't believe that the Islands were cruel to me; they were following the regulations that I'd violated. It didn't help that my aunt said that she wouldn't sleep until I was back home. Again, showing unwillingness to be responsible for consequences—to her and possibly to others, in this case, me. In perfect alignment with my behavior to date, I got caught and tried to say "Whatever" and shrug it off. Boy, was I to find out how stupid I was.

Esmeralda knew she was likely putting Hector at some risk by turning me in to the authorities, but she thought she could use that in her favor. She would be the good friend who stood by Hector through all of this and who would be there after whatever was to happen did. Anonymously outing the two of us was ridiculously easy. She called the local health department and let them know that she'd seen someone who was supposed to be in quarantine out and about. They said they'd take it from there, and they did.

Hector and I returned to my hotel after that day on the beach and at many parties. I said good night to him and reminded him I wouldn't see him for the next few days as I had exams to take. We kissed, and he walked away.

A uniformed and masked officer stepped out of the elevator and asked, "Claire McGinnis?"

"Yes," I replied. "Can I help you?" Standing in the hallway, I was technically in breach of the quarantine rules. I knew I could probably argue myself out of that, but I was still nervous about what this visit meant.

"You're not wearing your bracelet. Where is it, and where've you been?" the officer asked.

"It's in the room. I took it off earlier because it was hurting my wrist. My boyfriend just came by to see how I was holding up. And to say goodnight. I need to get back to studying for my exams," I said. I started to walk back to my room.

"Stay where you are, please. So, you've been studying all day?" the man asked.

Nervously, I thoughtlessly responded, "Off and on, yes. Otherwise, I've been sleeping and reading. Being under quarantine is not that exciting."

"I suppose it isn't. But it's necessary to protect our Island from the scourge of this disease," the officer said.

"I agree completely. That's why I've been complying with your directions that I fully understood I would need to comply with when I applied to come here," I said.

"Really? Ms. McGinnis, it might be better for you if you stopped talking. Come over here. I want to show you something," the man said.

I walked over toward him. Hector came with me, and the man said, "No. Wait right there, Mr. Artigas. I'll get to you in a moment."

When I was about six feet from the man, he said, "Stop right there." He handed me a mask and a pair of gloves. "Put these on." I complied, but I was sick to death at what I thought I was about to see.

"Now. Look," and he showed me a series of photos of Hector and me at the beach and the parties that day. It felt like that I'd had the breath knocked out of me.

"I'm placing you under arrest for violating quarantine and lying about it just now. You're very unlucky, young lady. Yesterday, a new COVID-19 quarantine law made the penalty for quarantine violation much clearer—and more severe. You're potentially liable for a two-year jail term and up to a $10,000 fine in U.S. dollars."

"Because you didn't immediately own up to the violation and take responsibility, I'm going to recommend that you and you, Mr. Artigas, be the first people tried under this new law."

"Both of you make me sick with your arrogance and disregard for others," said the officer.

He had us both turn around and face the wall. He zip-cuffed us both, and two more officers, one a woman, appeared and led us out of the hotel, through the lobby. They drove us to a government quarantine facility to spend the next two weeks in virtual, solitary confinement. I missed my exams because there was no Internet service in the facility, and, anyway, they would allow me to have none of my belongings until I tested negative at the end of the quarantine period.

I knew I was very far up shit's creek as we said in America, but also knew that I had brought this all on myself and Hector. I tried to envision what two years in prison here would be like and what it would mean to my life, but I couldn't. All I could see was a large black hole into which I had fallen.

| 2 |

My Stupid Actions Bear Bitter Fruit

December 5-8:

The quarantine facility was an old immigration detention center the Islands government had closed several years before. The new immigration facility, on the same grounds, looked comfortable, far more comfortable than our accommodations. I had to imagine that was intentional. Only evil people—quarantine violators—would be here. Ours was a two-story building; they housed men on the top floor and women on the first floor. Each cell, such as they were, was previously a 36-square foot cage to which they added frosted plexiglass walls to reduce the risk of transmission of the disease. Otherwise, though, it remained a cage. I mused: the Islands must have taken their lead on immigration detention facilities from the United States.

I spent the next two weeks in the cell, only to be removed from quarantine for trial and periodically for showers. There were four other women on my floor and only one other male up with Hector, all foreigners like me. I never saw any of them as there were few enough of us to use services like the showers and phone without ever seeing each other.

Probably no help for me, and our case was that one of the women and her boyfriend who was up with Hector contracted the disease. When they recovered, they were deported immediately. Likely the government felt that experiencing and surviving the disease was enough of a punishment. In any case, that made the local papers much more hostile to those of us in the facility, mainly me.

Our trial was scheduled to start on December 5th, five days after I arrived at the facility. In the meantime, I spent the time lying on my bed in the cell—an old shredded fiber-filled mattress that had seen better days. The air was stagnant and hot; there was no airflow because of the plexiglass separators. They left me in the clothes that they'd arrested me in. The quarantine facility didn't provide a thing in the way of toiletries, books, or entertainment of any kind. Once a day, I could go to the communal shower area—by myself—to attempt to clean off. They fed me twice a day by sliding a tray under the door to my cage. It was a spicy liquid with pieces of meat and vegetables in it. They called it Carne Guisada, but it didn't look like what I'd seen elsewhere using that name.

Daily, I could use the phone to call home, collect. I delayed calling until December 2nd because I was too embarrassed to talk to my parents. When I did, what I heard was a mixture of worry, relief, and rage about how stupid I'd been. They said that they'd heard from the hotel that I'd gone out the night of November 30th and had disappeared. They were worried sick. All they could think of was Natalee Holloway, the young woman who disappeared years before in Aruba, never to be seen again. They were angry about me not contacting them and now outraged at the way I was being treated. I was wise enough not to remind them they were fully aware of the trip and my intentions; the government monitored every conversation, said a sign above the phone. I tried to tell them that I had broken the law and violated an agreement I'd had with the government here, but they wouldn't listen.

On December 5th, a female officer came to my cage with an outfit from my suitcase. "We're heading out to the Court for your trial. Once we're done there, we'll come back here for the rest of your quarantine. Get dressed."

"Can I take a quick shower?" I asked.

"Yes, if you make it really quick. You don't want to keep the Court waiting," she said.

I jumped in and out of the shower, dried myself off, combed out my long hair to air dry, and dressed. I thanked the guard, who didn't say anything. She put a leather belt around my waist, cuffs on my hands, and manacles on my ankles. A chain attached the cuffs and manacles to the belt, so I had a minimal range of motion.

The guard led me out of the quarantine facility to a waiting car. Hector was already in it.

"You two are not to talk to each other. Just sit there quietly. The prosecution will ask us what you talk about, and us saying 'Nothing' would be the best thing for you," said the driver.

The belts we wore were chained to bolts in the seats, and we were seat-belted in. The ride was about half an hour. The car wasn't air-conditioned, and so by the time we reached the courthouse, I was sticky with sweat again. The guards led us into the courthouse, and they took me to a room where I met my court-appointed attorney, Anthony Hodgins, a junior associate at a local law firm. He told me about the procedure for the trial.

"The State will present their case first. I've seen their materials, and I have to say, you have little of a defense. The best thing for you would be to throw yourself on the mercy of the Court as you are a first offender, and you're a student-in-good-standing in the United States. If you're contrite and take responsibility for your actions, the State might be merciful. If you're aggressive or embarrass the State, they won't be," he said.

"What are your intentions?" he asked.

I was overwhelmed and asked, "Where's Hector?"

"He has his own counsel. A friend has taken care of that."

"What friend? I thought he and I were in this together?" I asked.

"I don't know. But you need to focus on your case, Claire. Don't worry about Hector," Hodgins said.

I said, "Throw me on their mercy, I guess. We—I—were stupid and irresponsible, and I'll take whatever the punishment is for that. I will tell you, Anthony, my biggest concern is the implications for my future as a lawyer. I know I'll miss school and have already missed my semester finals. Law schools will look at that and ask a lot of questions."

"Well, I think we ought to worry about that if and when it becomes an issue," he said.

"Now, as to the potential penalty. The State recently enacted some new regulations that cleared up some very foggy rules on penalties and early release. According to these new rules, any person incarcerated by a ruling from the Court you will see must serve only 60% of the sentence. In your cases, if they give you the full two years, that will mean that you would be out in about 14 months."

I felt like someone had hit me with a baseball bat—fourteen months in prison. My life was over; I knew it.

"You would be on parole here for the rest of the sentence, so another ten months and would have to hold down productive employment and see a parole officer, initially daily. You would also be subjected to random, unannounced drug and COVID tests, as you will be in jail. After that, Claire, you would be deported back to the U.S. and could not return until the State allows it. That might be 2-3 years. This is the worst that it could be. I don't see you not being punished, but I'm going to document your previous exemplary behavior and make a case for the lightest sentence possible," Anthony said.

We went into the Court; the entire process dizzied me. Given the difference with U.S. courts, I struggled to follow the proceedings. In the end, the Judge said, "Defendants, please rise. I've heard the evidence and your confessions and apologies and will consider all that has been said overnight. I'll render my sentence tomorrow. We incline our courts toward leniency, but in this case, I am not so sure, especially Ms. McGinnis, you being pre-law. You should have understood the importance of law for order and, particularly, in this case, our country's health. Because of behavior like yours, particularly from Americans, we recently enacted stiffer penalties for quarantine violation. Your arrogance and selfishness are symbolic of your country, as, I will say, is your sense of entitlement. I will take all of this into consideration when I consider my sentence."

I left the court crying. All I had heard was the judge would throw the book at Hector and me and that any opportunity for me to be a lawyer was dead. Again, and I only thought about this later, I had made this be all about me. What I might have done to others, particularly Hector, wasn't even a thought.

I didn't sleep that night. Once again, the following day, a jailer brought some clothes for me to wear and allowed me to take a quick shower. I went out to the car and found that Hector wasn't there. I didn't know what that meant, but I knew it couldn't be a good thing.

When I arrived at the Court, he wasn't there either. I asked Anthony. "He took a path to quick sentencing late last night. They gave him a 14-day sentence, and he has to pay a fine of about $500."

"What path was that?" I asked.

"That friend of his asked her father to intervene with the courts for Hector, and they asked the judge for separate sentencing. I'm sure they thought you would drag him down," said Anthony.

"What do you mean by that?" I asked. Anthony had confirmed what I was thinking about my chances.

"Well, I'm concerned myself. You heard the Judge yesterday. He directed most of what he had to say at you, well, Americans, I guess, but you are the American in the bullseye here. Also, there's been a veritable hue and cry from the U.S. about you, led by your maternal aunt. She's been on almost every media outlet and even gotten one of your President's sons to make some idiotic comments. It's the thing I wanted to avoid. Your family, and by implication, you, are embarrassing our country and courts. The judge may have no alternative but to sentence you under the new law to the maximum. But we will appeal; rest assured we will."

We went into the Court, and the judge delivered the sentence, "Ms. McGinnis, please stand. Your behavior here and complete disregard for our laws and our people's health leave me with no choice but to sentence you to the full term prescribed by law, two years, and levy a fine of $10,000, which will need to be paid before you leave the Island. Nineteen people are currently under quarantine because of you. If any of those comes down with the disease, I will reconsider the sentence in the light of that and may levy different judgments. We'll take you from here and return you to your quarantine center. From there, in five days, we'll take you to the women's facility on Shepherd's Island to begin your sentence. Mr. Hodgins, do you have questions?"

"Thank you, Your Honor. As I am sure you expected, we will appeal this sentence, which I feel is far too severe given Ms. McGinnis's background and contriteness. Second, I ask why did you choose the prison on Shepherd's Island? It's far away from principal population centers and is where we send the worst of our offenders. Wouldn't it make more sense to her to commit her to the custody of the city jail?"

"I fully expect that you will appeal, Mr. Hodgins," said the Judge. "You have every right to. I considered all the information delivered to me, including the depositions of the officers that arrested Ms. McGinnis, during which she was lying about her behavior. She does not seem to be particularly apologetic to me. I don't have to explain my choice regarding the sentence's location, but I'll tell you that the city jail is overcrowded and recently became a COVID-19 hotspot. I'm looking out for the good of Ms. McGinnis with this. One last thing, I'm sure that you know this, but the Court of Appeals is about to end its session for this year. You must move fast to get yourself on their docket. I can assist with that and send them the court documents and a request to schedule the case for next Tuesday. It's after the close of the session, but I think I can persuade them to hear you in a special session."

"Thank you, Your Honor," said Anthony.

"You're very welcome. The Court is adjourned."

I met with Anthony after the session. I felt suicidal. "What am I going to do, Anthony? I can't go to that place for two years. I won't survive. Anyway, my life is over. I just can't believe I was so stupid."

"Ms. McGinnis, I can't speak to your life after this, but there will always be a life after this. It's still up to you to make the best life. I, myself, was in a position not unlike yours, not a COVID-19 quarantine violation, but a theft when I was about your age. They sentenced me to two years in jail, and there I committed I would make myself the best person I could be. You can do the same if it comes to that," he said.

"I need to work on your petition to the Court of Appeals. The Judge did a good thing for us by agreeing to get them to hold a special session for us next week. Their last session for the year is tomorrow. You can do one thing for me," he asked. "Please get to your family and ask them to stop going to the media. The Appeals Court will be quite unlikely to change anything if your family doesn't stop. I also can't predict what will happen if your President or State Department tries to get involved. Plead with them to stop. I just hope it's not too late."

December 14-15:

Time passed slowly for me. For the next six days, I heard from Anthony every day, sometimes to ask a question, but most of the time, to see how I was doing and to try to keep my spirits up. As much as he tried, my spirits would not lift, though. I tried to get my parents to back off on the media several times, but they wouldn't. They believed what they were doing was for my benefit; they wouldn't listen to my pleas to stop. Toward the end, I began to think they might want to see me in prison. I also couldn't talk them into talking to my aunt to stop the media blitz. The State Department had tried to intervene and was told that this was an internal matter and that they should back off. I could only imagine what this was going to mean for me at my appeal.

Hector never called or tried to visit. I gave up on him, further deepening my depression.

On the morning of the 14th, a jailer brought me some clothing as on the previous trips to the Court. This time, Anthony provided them. A very sensible black suit with a white shell underneath it. It made me look serious, and he told me this: Showing I was serious, he believed, might persuade the Court of my remorse.

When I arrived at the Court, all I could see was a large field of reporters and media; my world started to come apart. NBC, CBS, CNN, ABC, Fox, Al Jazeera, and even One America broadcast live from the courthouse. One of the ONAN reporters shoved a microphone in my face and asked, "Could we get an interview with you, Claire. Your aunt asked us to reach out to you to get your side of this story, especially about your poor treatment by the Island government and courts."

Anthony stepped in and told them it was inappropriate to speak before the Court rendered their decision and that we'd be late if we didn't move on.

"I'm sorry, Claire, but the only way this could go worse for you would be if the reporters stormed the Court. The Judges are watching this, I'm sure, and all this negative coverage does is push them into a corner," said Anthony.

We walked into Court and the worst day of my life. Well, maybe there are worse days to come, but it was the worse up to now.

"All rise for this special session of the Court of Appeals. The Honorable Alice Sutton, Honorable Vernon Hodge, and Honorable Louis Little presiding."

The trio entered, and the bailiff said, "Please take your seats."

Judge Sutton spoke, "We gave careful consideration to the materials presented from the Magistrate's Court and reports from the local and international media. We must tell you all, they do not paint us as a civilized country and force us to most carefully weigh all the materials and the law in rendering our decision."

Judge Hodge picked up, "Our deliberations led us to conclude that the Magistrate's court erred in its decision."

I felt relieved. Maybe something would go in my direction.

He continued, "We, initially, concluded that the defendant was being treated too harshly, and we were, and I want to underscore, *were* planning to reduce the sentence to a year and a $2,500 fine."

With that, my good feelings evaporated.

The last of the trio, Judge Little, concluded, "However, this morning, the police gave us information that gave us pause and forced us to appreciate better the rationale for the legislature's creation of this new law. Four of the people on quarantine because they associated with Ms. McGinnis have now come down with COVID-19. Two are extremely sick and are on ventilators. So, our reconsideration of the sentence incorporates into it four additional counts of grievous bodily assault. The revised sentence is two years for violating the quarantine laws, but we have reduced the fine to $2,500, as previously mentioned. For the four assault counts, the sentence will be five years for each count, those sentences to be served concurrently, but after the quarantine violation. As noted before, you will serve your sentence at the Shepherd's Island Women's Prison and will be eligible for conditional release in about four years. Again, we reserve the right to revisit judgments if there are any changes in the conditions of the hospitalized, other people in quarantine, or their circles of family and friends."

"May I speak, your Honors?" asked Anthony.

"Of course, Mr. Hodgins."

"How do you attribute the illness of those four individuals to Ms. McGinnis?" asked Anthony.

"A good question," said Judge Sutton. "Some of this is, of course, circumstantial, but we base it on good intelligence and fact gathering by the Department of Health. First, no one else in these people's families or circles of friends has contracted or had the disease. Second, based on pictures we have seen of the events attended by Ms. McGinnis, they were all very close to her. The others being quarantined were much further away. Third, we take daily swabs from Ms. McGinnis at the quarantine facility. They have shown antibodies for the disease, which makes us believe she was an asymptomatic carrier. Finally, her social media touts the fact that she had the disease and was symptom-free. We realize that there is a fair amount of circumstantiality to this, and so, when we come back into session next year, we will review the status of her case, and if there is more or new information, we'll reconsider the sentences. In the meantime, if conditions change, we reserve the right to reconsider the sentences immediately. I will be monitoring all of these cases during our recess and will be back to you if any changes warrant a reevaluation of the sentences."

"Ms. McGinnis, we're sorry about this, but you have brought this on yourself by your irresponsibility and arrogance. We wish you the best and that you take this as a learning opportunity. Do you care to address the Court?" asked Judge Sutton.

"Yes. Thank you all. I realize that this is an extraordinary session of this Court, and I thank you for your allowing me this opportunity to persuade you as to my remorse. However, I understand I need to be punished for anything I might have done given what's happened. I feel you have been generous to me in many ways. I will make the best of the next years and the rest of my life. Again, thank you," I said as tears streamed down my face.

On the morning of the 15th, a transfer team took me to Shepherd's Island. Anthony told me it had been a slave plantation during the 1800s and turned into a prison after that. There were two complexes on the Island: a men's and women's prison and a men's and women's prison for Lifers. I didn't need to ask what those were, and given where I was and that two of the people infected were on ventilators, I knew I was a stone's throw from being in that second prison.

None of the Island's jails or prison facilities had good reputations. In fact, they were called "barbaric" in one internal audit report on conditions there. Their own people couldn't whitewash conditions. I guessed that was why Anthony questioned my being sentenced there when the sentence was much shorter. Now, there was only one place for me to go as an actual felon.

Most of the men's prisons and all the women's prisons were not air-conditioned and, during inclement weather, were subject to floods, loss of utilities, and other problems. Rats, snakes, and other vermin infested both the prisons and cohabitated with the prisoners. Anthony said that he'd seen pictures of the men's prison with water stains halfway up the first level wall from floods. He said the women's prison was just as bad. Also, to call Shepherd an island was being extremely kind to it. It actually was a raised piece of land in the middle of a large swamp. You got to it on an airboat or through the front gate; a small town that had grown up by the prison. Many staffers lived there.

The prison focused most prisoner activities on what they called upkeep. It was more like, Anthony said, the little Dutch boy and the dike. He said that he'd work hard to get me transferred out of prison as soon as possible and not to lose heart. I thanked him but had little more heart to lose.

"Thank you, Anthony. I know you've worked hard for me, and I deeply appreciate that. I'm here because of the stupid things that I did. I guess I deserve this. Please do nothing that puts yourself, your firm, or me at further risk. Also, reach out to my family and let them know what's happened and that they should stop trying to get me out. They're only making things worse," I said.

I could tell that Anthony felt awful for me, even though I brought this all on myself. He committed to himself to do the best he could for me.

That would take years and years, and a different, better person would emerge from imprisonment.

| 3 |

Shepherd's Island

The First 6 Months; Time Flies; Not:

Prisoner Intake for Shepherd Island processed me for Shepherd in the city jail annex because they didn't want me exposed to COVID-19 at the jail. Two guards from the prison were there, a man and a woman. They took my suitcases, backpack, and computer briefcase and gave me a receipt for them and, in return, gave me prison clothes. The Shepherd Island uniform was a set of black scrubs with my number embroidered on it. Splendid color for this heat, I thought.

"There are two sets of these uniforms. We'll keep one for you until it's time to change out of the one you're wearing. This number'll identify you from now on. You may as well forget you ever had a name, at least for the next," and he looked at his pad, "four-plus years," said the male guard. I looked down and saw my number was 56422.

The trip to the Island was long and uncomfortable. As with my other outings, I was chained, first to the seat of a car, then the back of a truck carrying supplies to the prison, and finally in one of several airboats that took us to the Island. The last part was frightening as the boat-driver seemed to revel in scaring me and saturating me with the fetid swamp water.

All of what followed was intended, I guess, to heap degradation on degradation, to acclimate me to what my life was going to be like for a least the next four years. At the end of it all, I was pretty sure that I wasn't going to survive, in one piece anyway.

When we arrived at the prison dock, they dragged me off and removed my chains. A guard said, "Well, Convict, you may as well get used to your life here. Unload those boats and put all the cargo in the back of that truck. Anything you can't fit in there, there's a wheelbarrow you can push up the track to the prison."

I did my work, and even with good packing on the truck, I had a large load of canned goods to load into the wheelbarrow and then push up into the prison. I was sweaty and filthy by the time I got there. My feet were a mess; they didn't give shoes or slippers to any prisoners, so mine were bare and now bruised and bloody. I suppose that they will toughen up over time.

They gave me a pillow, a blanket, and a few toiletries and told me they'd wash the clothes and blankets once a month at a cost to me. I got paid about a dollar a day for my work here. They could replenish the toiletries for a nominal fee as well.

The prison supplied women's sanitary products on request for no cost. Small favors, I guessed.

They then sent me to the next room for a medical examination. Routine lab samples were taken, and they gave me yet another COVID-19 test.

"I just had one yesterday and tested negative. That's how I got on the boat to make the trip here," I said.

"Don't mouth off, Convict. We're testing everyone here, every day. If you come across positive or inconclusive at any point, we'll place you in quarantine, which in our case is our hole. You'll have time to see that during your orientation tour," said the guard.

"Now, when did you have your last period?" asked the nurse.

"I'm having it now," I said.

"Excellent. Male and female convicts mix frequently, and as you can see, most of the guards here are males, even in the female prison. We give each female convict a birth control implant for your safety and health. It works for five years, and you can start trading for favors as soon as I install it. Lift your arm. This is going to hurt. In normal circumstances, we offer an anesthetic shot before the implant, but these are not normal circumstances, and you're not a normal recipient of this benefit," said Nurse Wretched.

She took the implant out of a silver foil package and displayed it to me; she jammed it into my forearm. I howled with the sudden pain. I thought she got some sadistic pleasure out of hearing me scream.

"Will there be any side effects?" I asked. "Also, what did you mean 'trade for favors'?"

"Need to know, Convict, need to know, and you don't need to know about any side effects. If I have to tell you what I mean about trading, you're dumber than I thought. You'll find out soon enough. Now move on to the next room to see the barber."

"Barber? I don't need a haircut," I complained.

"Every convict gets a haircut. It makes the start of your day much easier, and it can't get messed up in your work."

They ushered me roughly into the next room, where there was a barber chair with wrist and knee restraints. The guard forced me onto the chair, tightened the bonds, and left me to the barber, a large man.

"My oh my, you are a beauty," he said, "I'm going to enjoy this." He produced a large cutter and, with no ceremony, cut hair from my head, leaving me looking like the Little Dutch Boy whose fingers were in the dike. Poetic justice, I guess. When he was finished, he said, "Don't you look the wonder. Not the pretty little beach babe anymore, huh?"

With that done, the guard returned; he laughed at me. "Now you look like the rest of the prisoners, 56422. Let's go to the blacksmith." I didn't bother reacting to that right away, knowing that whatever I would do wouldn't prevent what was about to happen.

The blacksmith was the real thing. "You'll be here a minimum of 49 months according to your record," and he gestured toward a PC in the shop's corner, "So, I programmed this," and he held up a curved piece of metal, "for that amount of time. If you end up spending more time here or move around to another prison location, I'll reprogram you." He walked over to me.

When I saw what he was about to do, I resisted despite my earlier thoughts. The guard grabbed me and pinned my arms to my chest so I couldn't, and the blacksmith brought the metal to my neck and closed the collar. With that snap I heard, I saw my newest disgrace.

"This will only unlock with a special secure app that we don't have access to here. Look at it as the State giving you some nice jewelry. The collar also has etched into it your prisoner number. That's to ID you if we only find your skeleton somewhere. There's also a geo-tracker in it; I understand that you've some experience with one of those. This one won't slip off." He did finger quotes when he said "slip."

"It's set to allow you to move into specific areas of the prison. You violate the rules, it will beep at you, like this," and it beeped, "and if you continue to break the rules, you'll get an unpleasant shock." A substantial shock hit me and knocked me off the bench. "That's half of what you get if you break the rules and don't come back inside bounds, just to give you a picture of what might happen to you." He and the guard laughed at me sitting there on the floor.

"By the way, Convict, most of you pee on yourself when I hit you with that second shock. You didn't. That means that you're stronger than most. You'll need to be," said the blacksmith.

The guard led me into the prison to my cell, the last one down a long corridor with cells on either side. No cell opposite mine, though. Privacy? Or, what? Between my cell and the next was a maintenance closet. The cell was small, maybe four feet wide and eight feet deep, smaller than my cell at the quarantine facility and what would be my home for the coming years. It had a small bed, like that I had in quarantine, and with the same shredded fiber mattress, a steel toilet, and a fold-down writing desk I could use from the bed. A few hooks were on the wall for clothes.

They fed prisoners twice a day, once at 6 AM and again at 6 PM. In between, they assigned prisoners to two work details, plugging the dike. Mine was going to be the kitchen and farm. I was told my day would begin at 4 AM with the kitchen assignment and end at 8 or 9 PM. From 9 AM until 4 PM, I would join teams working in the fields. These were male and female prisoner teams closely monitored by guards with shotguns, some on horses. If I'd known something about horses, I might have been assigned to the stables. I heard that was a cushy posting if you liked shoveling manure. The last hours every day would be back in the kitchen.

We grew almost all our vegetables and cotton for clothing on the farm. The farm teams tilled the soil using convict-pulled plows, fertilized, maintained, and picked produce and cotton. Everyone got a chance at both ends of the plows, which meant during the growing seasons—and there were three each year—I got to pull the plow once a week early in each season. Over the months between my work in the kitchen, primarily as a scullery maid, and my work on the farm, I developed significant upper arm and leg strength. Days when I went to sleep sore were now few. As I looked at the shower mirror and saw my muscle development, I thought that I began to look like a mule or an ox, like a beast, but in a good way.

My cell was formerly part of the maintenance closet, hence its smaller dimensions than the average cell and its isolation from the others. I had many nighttime visitors consequently. After staying in the hole for two days, I realized that it wouldn't help me survive the ordeal to resist.

Four months into my first year, a guard took me to the Warden's office. "Good afternoon, Convict. Judge Sutton and your attorney would like to see you in a video courtroom session." He took me to a conference room off his office, saw that they locked my wrist chains to a bolt in the center of the conference table, and then waited until the Judge and Anthony appeared on the screen. The Warden adjusted the volume and then left the room. As he did, I saw him shake his head, I thought, sadly.

Both the Judge and Anthony looked grim. "Good afternoon, Ms. McGinnis. I'm afraid that we don't have good news for you. We understand one of the two people who contracted COVID-19 because of exposure to you, and Mr. Artigas was taken off ventilation today and died. That means that one of your assault charges has now been amended to murder."

I sat back completely shocked, and started to cry.

"The sentence for murder is ninety-nine years in prison, so for all intents and purposes, life. Our laws don't allow for any other sentence. I'm deeply sorry about this as I've taken a great personal interest in your case," said the Judge.

"Ms. McGinnis, the Judge wants to make an offer to you, though. You'll remember that you must serve 60% of your sentence. In your case, you would be eligible for parole in sixty years," said Anthony.

"Stop. I don't want to hear anything more. Warden! I'm ready to return to my cell," I wept.

"Please wait, Claire," said Anthony. "Listen to what Judge Sutton wants to offer. She wants to help if she can. She was serious about her concern. She's gone way out on a limb for you."

When the Warden and the guard came back into the conference room, I waved them away. They left, but not before the Warden pushed a box of tissues toward me. I thought that might mean that he was a good guy. I was to find, though, he was anything but that.

"We can't release you before some significant time has passed," said the Judge, "but have agreed to allow your conditional release to parole in 20 years if you agree to become a spokesperson for the State on taking our quarantine rules seriously. This would entail radio, social media, print, TV, and other spots and your willingness to take interviews from news services in which you talk about your offense, what it has done to your life, and the life of the deceased and his family. We also want you to talk about how the State has treated you fairly.

You must convincingly state you hold yourself completely responsible for where you find yourself. If you do all of this, we will show our gratitude by giving you early parole."

I thought about that, "A couple of questions, Judge: Is Hector facing the same sentence as me, and will he be taking part in these shamings? Second, what do you mean by public interviews? How will those be done with me here?"

"Regarding Hector, we have charged him with murder as well, but he left the country with his new wife before we levied the charge. Her father was well-connected and heard about the man's death before the police could act. He's in another country that doesn't have extradition to us. If he ever travels here again, he'll be arrested instantly. He's being tried *in absentia* as we speak," she said.

"Regarding the public interviews, we want you to appear with the family of the deceased to take full responsibility for what happened to their family member. I imagine it will be an unpleasant interview, but you'll not be physically together with them to avoid any chances of assault. Several of your TV networks have also been asking for interviews with you, and we want you to do them as well. We'd give you the questions they'd ask and the parameters for your responses as well. We desperately want to reset our reputation worldwide from the damage that your family has done to it. It would be my—our—expectation that you'd set that record straight," she finished.

"Just who is Hector's wife, Judge? If you don't tell me, I'll find out, anyway," I said.

"Esmeralda Vélez."

"That bitch!" I yelled, trying to rise out of my seat. The door behind me flew open, and the Warden and the guard came in. Both pressed me back down in my chair.

"It's all right, Warden." The men both left the room when I said that I was. "Are you settled down now, Ms. McGinnis?" asked Judge Sutton.

"Judge, thank you for telling me. I always thought she looked at Hector like she owned him and hated me. I just wish I could get my hands on them," I said."

"It's okay to say that in front of us, Ms. McGinnis, but not outside of here. Do you understand? If someone were to take that seriously, there'd be nothing I could do for you, especially if anything ever happened to either of them," said the Judge.

"Besides," she said with a brief smile, "I see the outside work that you've been doing has suited you well. You look extremely healthy. You would be a formidable opponent."

"Thank you, Judge. Life is hard, as I am sure you can imagine, but I'm getting through it. So, what do we do next?" I asked.

"Do you accept the offer, Ms. McGinnis? If yes, Mr. Hodgins and I have already drafted an agreement that you would need to sign. The Warden has it. If you do, we will start scheduling the media spots, interviews, and the other things we talked about. Again, I expect the interview with the family to be brutal for you, but I'll help you get through that. One thing that I want to do right away, assuming you agree and sign the agreement, is to get our media team out to you to do some photoshoots. We want to create a website that features you to emphasize the importance of compliance with the regulations. We also want to create several billboards that we'll place on the highways outside of the airports and marinas and ship terminals. Your face will become very well known quite soon."

"Not the way was in which I hoped, but I'm willing to do this," I said. I was thinking about everything I had suffered here already and what the next twenty years would bring. "This is the life I've handed myself, and I guess I have to go with it."

"Warden!?" He came through the door. "I'm ready to sign the documents."

I signed the papers, and they made a copy to be kept in my file in the prison records office. The Warden then said, "Now that your status has changed, you're going to be moved to a different location. You'll also have a different job assignment and number. As a Lifer, you'll get certain privileges if you play by the rules. If you don't, you'll lose the privileges and maybe suffer additional punishment. Do you understand, Convict?"

"Yes, Sir. I do. Where am I going?"

"Come over here to my window." He pointed out a long, low building on the inside of several high, barbed wire-topped fences. "There. It doesn't look like much, but it will be your home until we release you. There are currently 14 other women in that prison. You each have your own cell. They're better appointed than the ones here. You'll have complete freedom inside the buildings and those grounds, twenty-four hours a day, if you follow the rules and work out well in your new jobs. There's a store over there that has all things the store here does and then some. Finally, because you're a guest for many years to come, we'll supply you with all the personal toiletries that you'll need. Questions, Lifer? You'll note we've promoted you, so to speak. I know that you have got an agreement with the Judge on your sentence, but as far as anyone here is concerned, you're responsible for the death of one of our citizens, so a Lifer."

"I do have a question, Sir. I have a very isolated cell here and have come to like it. Is there any chance that I could get something like that over there?" I asked.

"The Lifer prison is currently holding 14 women. There's space there for 50. I'm sure we can find you something sufficiently isolated there. The bottom line is, over there, you have more freedom to do what you like, and so do the guards. If that is what you were asking about." And, I was. While I found some of what I had become accustomed to debasing, it also allowed me to get some human contact that I would otherwise be without. I was to find, though, the life in the Lifer prison would be more exciting and fulfilling.

They led me back to the uniform room, where I got my new Lifer uniform. It was a bright, almost fluorescent green, and my new number was number 32. The shirt was wider cut across the shoulders, revealing the tops of my breasts.

"What an ugly color," I said as I wondered about the way the shirt was cut. I didn't have long to find out why it was that way.

"The better to see you with, my dear," chuckled the guard. "You can have another one of these whenever you want it. Every Lifer gets their own Guard. I'm yours. My name is Sir to you. Understand?"

"Yes, Sir. What about anything else I might need?"

"Everything else you need will be in your cell. You're going to be in cell 46... Huh...Interesting, you're quite far away from the other Lifers. Does this mean you're going to be a problem?"

"No, Sir. I'm very compliant. Ask my old guards. They'd probably say I was submissive," I said.

"Well, don't let that get around here. These are the toughest customers on the grounds. Murderers mostly, but not like you. They'll probably have something to say to you about that. No fights.... You get into one, and you'll find yourself in the basement solitary. The solitary makes the prison hole look like the Ritz. You get a month for the first fight, then longer times after that. Understand?" he said.

"Yes, Sir."

"By the way, you don't impress me as being the typical dumb bitch we get here. Are you smart?" he asked.

"I thought I was once, but what I did to get me here told me I'm not. I'm getting just what I deserve," I said.

"Some of us think you're not. You're regretful, I get it, but we will have lots of years together to see how honest that is. Here's your cell. Look, and then I'll show you around some more," the Guard said.

After I looked around the cell, which was twice as large as my old one, he showed me the dining hall. It looked a lot like the dining hall in my old cell block. The kitchen, though, had much newer equipment. "This will be one of your worksites. The way we do work here is that you will have jobs every day, no days off. Your employment, like everyone else's, will have some outside work and some inside work. Your inside work will be in the kitchens, where you'll get training to be a station cook. You'll learn to make fast food types of meals and a few other things. This skill will be important when you get out if you ever do, as few places will hire an ex-con like you for anything requiring more brains than that. You'll also have an inside job cleaning up some rooms in the basement. It'll give you a chance to see one of the other things we do here. Your outside jobs will be working in the fields, not farming, but expanding them. We'll assign you to a male-female team and sometimes work you for several days at a stretch in the swamp, draining and clearing it—hot and dangerous work. You'll also work digging new trenches around the camp to channel the runoff from our storms. When there is a storm or a hurricane, you'll also be on a clean-up crew, maybe here, but most times back in the cities, depending on how bad things are there. We had a team there for two months after that last big hurricane and another there nearly six months after that monster tropical storm two years ago. We get endless kudos from the businesses here for the work that you all do. Kudos to our well-trained staff. I am sure you'll want to keep that up, right?"

"Yes, Sir. Of course, Sir."

"You get paid for all of this work. Not much, maybe two of your dollars an hour, and it is deposited into an account we manage for you. We'll deduct some of your expenses from that, but the rest are available for use in the store. If anyone sends or gives you money, we expect it to be deposited into that account. Understand?"

"Yes, Sir," I said.

"My understanding is that you also have some media obligations, correct?" he asked. I nodded. He kept looking at a small tablet that he carried in a holster on his belt. "I see you looking at this thing. They're brand new and keep us in constant contact with the communications center. It'll also play music if I want to listen to anything. Is there a kind of music that you like?"

"Yes, Sir. I'm a fan of *First Aid Kit* and Natalie Merchant. Most classical, I like too. Have you ever heard of Lindsey Stirling? She plays an incredible violin. And yes, I know about my media obligations. I'm not looking forward to them."

He told me he'd see what he could find for music from the artists I gave him as we walked. I was a little surprised because he seemed to be pretty much an iceberg otherwise. I thanked him. He got to like Lindsey Stirling, though he started off thinking she was a little too New Age for him.

"Judge Sutton has a media team here now, and they want some pictures of you. They said they want to see you working, so we'll meet them around back. I'll also let you know when other events are scheduled, but for right now, we'll head out back so you can dig your grave," he said.

I paused, shocked, when he said that. He looked at me carefully. "Lifers never leave here," he said. "You live and die here in prison. When you do, you're thrown into the grave you get to dig." I began to tear up. "Stop that. You have to get used to this. It's your life now." I couldn't see how I would or how this was life.

There were five media people, a couple of them with cameras out in the back of the Lifer Unit. The Guard took me to the graveyard. I saw a small field of simply numbered headstones. There were several, I observed, numbered 32. Two male convicts stood next to another stone numbered 32, and one held a shovel. He stuck it in the ground and walked away. The other threw a pair of pieces of wood at me, and he, too, walked away.

I'd seen the wooden pieces before but not tried them out; I would have if I stayed in the other prison much longer, I supposed. The slats of wood had large rubber bands mounted on them. You fit your feet through them to make a—very—primitive pair of sandals, tailored to make digging more efficient. I slipped them on and picked up the shovel.

My Guard said, "They'll take pictures and then ask you some questions about how it feels to be digging your own grave. I suppose it's gonna feel creepy. When you die, we pitch you in the hole and then fill it in. No words, no graveside service, just pitch you in. We then recycle your number. No one will ever know where you ended up. Something else to think about."

I dug for several hours non-stop, making the hole larger and larger and deeper and deeper. The soil was soft but heavy with moisture from the nearby swamp, I guessed. The sweat rolled off me. The media group leader said something to the guard, and he said, "Certainly," then turned to me. "They want you to get some dirt on your face and hands, so maybe you dig with your hands for a while. Give me the shovel, and you can take off those sandals."

I did and then got down on my hands and knees and continued to dig. I was filthy to my elbows, and my clothes were soiled and clung to my body. Lines of dirt flowed down my face with the sweat.

"Excellent," said the media person. "32, come over here... now."

It shocked me to hear my number called like that for the first time and ordered like a dog; another piece of my dignity flushed away. I walked over to the edge of the hole. I was at nearly 6 feet as far as I could tell, and the guard confirmed that. "Climb on out of the hole," he said and laughed after I tried unsuccessfully to get out a few times.

"You jump, and I'll pull." The guard handed me the shovel handle. I scrambled up with his help.

"These are some magnificent pictures, 32. They'll look good on the billboard and website we're planning. The theme will be 'You, too, could find yourself here if you don't follow the rules.' No one will know your name, though you are famous in some circles, infamous in others. Nope, the billboards and postings will all say, 'I am Lifer 32. I used to be like you.' Then the rest. Like that?"

"It'll be powerful, ma'am," I said.

"Glad you think so. Now, we've brought along some recording gear, and we want you to talk about who you are and what got you here. Just let it flow out, and we'll edit it together. We'll probably be back tomorrow to show you mockups of some things."

As they set up the equipment, the media leader continued to talk to, well, anyone who'd listen. I looked on, playing that I was attentive, though I was deeply hurt, confused, and angry—mostly at myself for agreeing to this.

"You know, as you were digging, 32, you made me think of an old song by Joni Mitchell. Do you remember the *Magdalene Laundry?* There were some great lines in there, especially about how they just shoved girls that died into a hole with no words. Kind of like what will happen to you here, 32," she said as she gestured at my hole. "Maybe I'll see if we can get rights to use the song on the website."

I could come to hate this woman.

The Guard looked at her like she was crazy, and I thought he might say something. Likely not in front of me, but maybe he would.

They set up the equipment and brought out lemonades for everyone except me. The guard winked at me. The questioning lasted for almost two hours, focusing on the damage I'd done to myself and my family by not following the rules. They focused on the plans I'd had and how, now, all of those were dashed by my behavior. I was told to say, several times, in several ways, that this was all my responsibility, that I had been arrogant and unfeeling, deserved this punishment, and was deeply sorry for all that I'd done to people. They made me feel like the rotten bitch they wanted me to appear to be. I said that the State had no other recourse but to punish me as they have and would be doing. One other thing they made me voice in a few ways was, "Don't waste your life as I'm wasting mine." By the end of the interview, I was a wreck, emotionally and physically. Pictures they took while I was being pilloried, the media leader said, would look great on the website and in the public service announcements they were developing.

When they left, the guard walked me over to my hole. "Usually, what we do is have the new Lifer spend her first night in the hole, but before we do that, I want to take you downstairs." He also handed me a lemonade.

"Don't tell anyone I gave you this," and he smiled kindly at me. "I know this is all tough for you. I may not be that sympathetic to you based on what you did, but I am for you as a person."

We walked through the door we had exited before and down a flight of stairs accessed through a keyed gate. "We'll give you a key to this. Not because we trust you, but because any failure in keeping this area secure will be your responsibility, and you'll be badly punished. Understand?"

"Yes, Sir. You can trust me," I said.

"I don't and never will. When you see this place, you'll keep your mouth shut all on your own," he said.

The door opened into a well-lit corridor that stank of sweat, and what I would find out was blood, fear, excrement, and sex. He took me to a room, opened the door, and then turned on some lights, stepping back and ushering me in. The room was brightly lit by large klieg lights built into the ceiling and on stands. Behind the lights were a couple of rows of seats, and behind that was a large one-way mirror. It was what was in front of the light stands that transfixed me. X-shaped wooden frames, benches, and tables with worn leather straps on them and, on the walls, hooks with many torture instruments hanging there.

"You ever heard of the Security Cooperation Agreement? It's a program of the U.S. government and a successor to some older cooperative programs where security officers got training in rendition fine arts, they call it. They bring terrorist suspects here to be interrogated. Your job will be to clean up the mess. I'll tell you now; it can be pretty revolting."

"I'll be with you the first few times you're working here to help you through it. It makes you pretty hard, I have to tell you," said the Guard.

I walked around the area, bug-eyed, with horror.

Finally, he looked at his watch and said, "Time to get you something to eat and for you to get some sleep."

We walked up to my hole, and I saw two things. There was now a chain running down into the hole. Attached to the end of it was a padlock with a set of keys in it. Someone had put this in while we were downstairs.

"Excellent," said the guard. "Go over there, 32."

"Yes, Sir." I walked over to the side of the hole and looked down. They had connected the chain to a metal stake driven into the ground at the bottom of the hole.

"I want you to pick up the chain, unlock the padlock, and give me the keys... Thanks... Now, I want you to tightly wrap the loose end of the chain around your ankle. Very good. Now lock the end of the chain to that link right there. Excellent."

He came up next to me and pushed me, so I flopped down to the bottom of the hole. "I'll be right back," he said. I thought he might say something glib, like, "Don't go away," but he didn't. I guess he knew how hard all of this was. He left for a few minutes and came back with a paper bag that had a grease stain on its side. There was a bottle of water in his hand as well. "Here's your dinner." And he threw the bag into me. He followed that with the bottle. "Eat up before the rats get to you."

"Yes, Sir."

I felt like I was going to puke.

"As I said before when you die, you'll be brought out here and dumped into the hole. Then, we shovel dirt on you: no words, no ceremony, nothing. Also, we'll re-use your number, so no one will ever know where you are. There are at least four other 32s buried here right now. I want you to think about what it will be like being here for all eternity tonight. We'll talk about that in the morning. Not unusual, as you know, but we're supposed to have some rain later. At least you'll be getting something more to drink."

He stayed with me until it rained, one of our regular downpours, and then left. He told me later that he had felt bad for me. I looked lost, and this was only the beginning for me.

It was an eternal night. I couldn't sleep. The one time I started to, I heard and then felt something jump into the pit. In the reflected light from the buildings, I saw an enormous rat looking at me. I stood up and moved to the opposite corner of the grave, far away from the food remains, leaving the rat, and then several more, to feast.

The rain stopped eventually, but there were about 6 inches of water in the grave's bottom and more leaking from the walls. I guessed that 6 feet down was extremely close to the water table here in the swamp. The only good thing, I thought, was that the next time down here, I wouldn't know or care about what I slept in.

The Guard came back after sunrise when the air had already become like a pressure cooker. "Did you have a good night? Did you think about my question?"

"Yes, Sir. I thought about it a lot."

"So?"

"I felt horror at first, but then realized that by the time that event occurred, I'll no longer care or know what's happening," I said.

"That's correct, but this night will stay with you always, and I hope it does, remaining in the back of your mind every day," he said, I thought with a note of sympathy.

He threw me a rope and helped me out of the grave. "You stink. I'll take you in for a shower. I got you some new scrubs. They're on your bed. When you're done, I need to take you to the blacksmith's shop to reprogram your collar so that you can travel out into the swamp on work details. After that, it's off to the kitchen for your first cooking lessons, and later today, there'll be the media folks. You've also got an interrogation today, and you gotta be downstairs after that."

"Sir, can I ask you a question?"

"Okay, go ahead."

"You know, and I know I'll be here for Life. Well, maybe 20 years, but that's life when you think about it. Don't you think that preys on my mind just by itself?"

"I suppose so, but what are you asking?"

"I'm asking you to try to be kind. I've fucked up my life and know it. I wake up every day knowing it. Being here," and I gestured around, "rams that home every second of every day. You could be a little kind to me."

He stopped walking and stared at me for a few seconds. "You're too damned forward for your good, do you know that?" he asked and then walked away.

I wasn't sure how to take that.

He took me back to my cell block and told me to take a shower and that he'd be back in an hour or so. I walked down to my cell to get my towel and the clean clothes. When I entered it, I found a tall, buff woman lying down on my bed. She opened one eye and lazily sat up. I was a big girl, but this girl was a muscular giant, not an ounce of fat, and very pretty. I was a bit apprehensive, remembering what the Guard had said about the inmates here.

"You're the new fish, aren't you?" she asked.

"Yes, I'm 32."

"Real names, Fish. Just because they take away who we are doesn't mean that we have to," the woman said.

I smiled, and though I was still a little apprehensive about the woman, I thought I might like her. "My name's Claire, Claire McGinnis," and I stuck my hand out.

"Mine's Paola Velasquez." She took me by my hand and pulled me down to the bed next to her. I saw the number 8 on her uniform.

"You've been here quite a while?" I asked.

"Yeah. So far, 18 years, basically since they opened the place. I killed my boyfriend and a friend of his who was using and beating me. Unfortunately, the friend was the son of a big-wig here on the Island, so here I am. And they've made sure that I ain't ever going anywhere except into the grave I dug for myself 18 years ago. You dug yours yet?"

"Yesterday, yes. I spent the night in it last night."

"Sadistic sons of bitches these guys are, and the Warden's the worst. There's a new guy who I kind of like, but most of the rest are pricks. Watch out for them."

She stood up, towering over me, and said, "You smell like a garbage dump. Come on; I'll help you shower."

"Paola, I've done nothing with a woman before. I'm not sure…," I said.

"What are you thinking, bitch, that I'm going to rape you or something? I enjoy doing it with women but remember what got me in here. I ain't ever going to force someone to do something they don't want to do. There isn't anyone here who'll do that. Come on. Despite what the screws will tell you, it's them you gotta watch out for," she said.

We walked down to the shower and took one together. After Paola scrubbed my back, I decided I couldn't spend the next 20 years fighting this, and so I didn't.

And so began a beautiful friendship—and more.

One thing that Paola taught me some time later was how to fight. The prison had approved purchasing and installing a boxing ring and much of the equipment needed to train and box, mixed martial arts style. Paola was an MMA whiz and thought that I would develop into a good sparring partner. So, she taught me. It was tough going at first for me as I'd done nothing like this before. But, because of my work in the fields, I was in pretty decent shape. Paola helped to develop me and found that I was almost a natural for the sport. When I was younger, I'd taken dance classes, so fight movements were easy to learn. What slowed me at first was that I didn't want to hurt anyone, so I laid off with my punches and kicks. Paola soundly thrashed me a few times, and I became more open to fighting back and eventually going on the attack. I began winning occasional bouts against Paola and then consistently, ultimately. To Paola's surprise and disappointment. Years later, we would still be sparring, though—and she would still be losing.

After my shower and time with Paola, the Guard and I walked to the blacksmith's shop. He used a small handheld device to reprogram my collar to allow me to travel out into the swamp to work and then told me to pull down my pants and take off my shirt. I looked at the Guard, and he told me to do it. The blacksmith told me to lie down on the bench, chest up.

"All Lifers get brands on two places on their bodies with their number on it, your left hip, like's done with other cattle and your right tit, like's done with slaves. The one on your tit will be readily observable to anyone that looks at you. Now you see why your uniform is designed how it is. Now hands over your head and don't move."

He took a small iron out of the fire and burned the number "3" into my tit. I hissed and teared up. He then did the same with the number "2". Again, I hissed and teared up. But, to their surprise, I didn't move. Both men looked at each other and smiled.

"Now, roll over. Be careful not to stretch the tissue on your chest. It'll hurt more if you do. Now the hip," said the blacksmith.

He applied the numbers "3" and "2" on my left hip and then put an insignia brand that showed I was an Island prisoner, a Lifer, on my chest and hip. With that done, they stood me up and told me to get dressed and gave me a drink of juice to prevent me from going into shock. Then the Guard walked me to the kitchen for my first day of line cook training. He left when the training cook talked about flipping burgers, being the only thing dumb convicts like I could do if I ever got out of prison.

Hours later, the Guard reappeared. I had just finished a round in the back room of the kitchen with the head chef. I walked like I was in pain. "You're hurting?"

"Only a little. He's not a patient lover, and I'm not at 100% because of the branding," I said.

"Your mistake is thinking that was love," he said. "It's not and never will be. Pure and simple, it's animal subjugation and degradation. If you get that, then the actions will be more tolerable. It never will be painless, but it'll help to get you through the next years."

"The media crew is back," he said, "and they want to show you their work. I think it looks fairly good. It makes you look like a scared and trapped brat, someone who'll suffer for what she's done for the rest of her life. We're going to the Warden's office."

We walked into the Warden's conference room where he, the media lead person, and several other people, some of whom I'd seen before, sat. They looked up when we entered, and the Warden told me to stand against the wall in the back of the room. He'd told them I'd received my brands today, and they wanted to get some pictures of them for a documentary they'd decided to do as well.

"Strip," said the Warden.

I hesitated a second, shrugged, and then pulled the shirt up over my head. I amazed myself at what I'd come to accept. There were several hisses of disbelief. I dropped my pants and then kicked them to the side. I modeled my brands for them. "Very nice. These will look good superimposed on that picture we have from your school gym locker room." I looked up, shocked, and the woman said to me, "It's amazing what you can get when you're willing to spend a little money. You also don't have a lot of friends back at home. Now stand there while we get some pictures."

They took the next few minutes up, snapping pictures and shoving me around to get them. If I could have felt humiliation, I would have, but I'd given up on that human emotion. I let them move me around like the cattle I was rapidly becoming. The Guard stood watching with what I took to be an angry look in his eyes.

"Good. Now we'll show you a few of the media spots we've made and the mock-ups of the billboards and flyers we put together. Don't bother with the clothes," the leader of the group said. "We want to catch your reactions to the spreads."

Again, the media spots were humiliating, but I'd agreed to this, and so I knew I had to suck it up. That said, I teared up a few times. The photographer even got a few of those moments and said to the rest, "These'll look great on that piece we're planning to do on remorse."

In the spots, they'd added some clips from friends, my parents, and my aunt. One of my friends said, "I'm not surprised that this happened to Claire. She always thought she was above the rest of us and didn't have to play by the rules. She's getting all she deserves as far as I'm concerned." A few others echoed similar sentiments. Most surprising was my former boyfriend, who called me an arrogant bitch who he always knew would take a significant fall. The photographer got more pictures of my anger and disappointment.

"We'll make sure we edit out your name on the spots we develop, but there's nothing we can do about what your friends back in the U.S. chose to do with them," said the media leader. I saw myself all over social media.

The billboards were as bad—for me—as the other media spots. I couldn't imagine what people would think day in and day out as they drove toward the city and vacation spots. "We'll make sure that you get the reviews of these. They might help in your rehabilitation," said the media leader.

I laughed out loud. "You don't understand a thing, do you? There's no rehabilitation for me. I know this is all part of a sentencing agreement I signed, but I don't expect to make it for 20 years and if I do, what I am being rehabilitated to do is to flip burgers in some dive or chain restaurant."

They left soon after that, with the media folks a little cha-grined and the Warden angry. I could have cared less. When the Guard said that he thought I might have lost it a little, I replied, "Sue me. What the Hell are they going to do to me that isn't being done already?"

"Hey, are you going to be around all the time?" I asked.

"Pretty much, yes. You're in my charge, though I'm not sure how long that'll be if you keep acting out in front of the Warden like that," he said.

"Well, sorry about that. Let me know if something looks like it will happen, and I'll try to help. You shouldn't have to suffer for my mouth. " I said.

"If I would consider it was suffering," he said.

I looked at him curiously.

"With you, I know what I get. I wouldn't know with some-one else. So, I think I'd rather stick with the rude bitch," he said with the hint of a smile.

"Anyway, if we're going to be spending all this time to-gether, can I get your name?" I asked.

"I told you that, it's Sir to you."

"Seriously," I asked.

"We're not supposed to give away personal details, and names are first on the list. You need to understand that you don't have rights anymore, especially the right to respect. You lost that when you didn't respect us," the Guard said.

That crushed me. I'd thought that a relationship had begun between us. We walked on.

"By the way, here's your key to the basement. That'll get you in through the door we entered last night, but you can't get out that way. In fact, once you're down there to work, you can't get out until I or someone else comes to get you. That means when you go down there, you must let me know you're going there. Understand?" he said.

"Yes, Sir."

He handed me the key. It was on a length of a heavy chain necklace, and I put it around my neck and dropped it inside my shirt.

"How do your tits and ass feel?" he asked conversationally.

"Okay, Sir. They burned for a few minutes after the branding, and then when I was standing over the broiler for three hours, but it gradually went away. I'm fine now."

"Good. We're here. Come with me to the Gown Room."

"Gown Room?"

"You'll see."

We walked down the hall, and he told me the key he'd given me would also open the door to the Gown Room. In it, we found a series of lockers, a shower, and some wash bins. They had labeled one locker "32." I wasn't sure how long it would take me to get used to that was the way everyone here would know me from now on. It always shook me when someone called my number, and now I saw it like this. I felt more and more of the old me slipping away from me day by day. It made me sad, but I also knew that I had no one else to blame. The accomplished submissive, I guessed.

"Okay. Strip and put on the gown you see hanging in there and those sandals," said the Guard.

I did. It was less a gown and more a potato sack with arm holes in it. "You have several jobs when you're here. Like I said yesterday, you'll clean the rooms after the interrogations. They get messy. I'll show you where all the cleaning stuff is. You'll also launder the clothing of the interrogators they put it into these bins. The laundry is back here. I'll show you how to get blood out of the clothes without ruining them. There will be a lot. Once the laundry is done and dried, you'll also iron the uniform shirts and pants and put them back in the correct lockers." We left the Gown Room and walked back out into the hallway. "The last thing you do, and this may be the grisliest part of your job, is to clean out the furnace that's back behind this door. That's where they burn the bodies when the interrogations are done."

"You're kidding, right?"

"Not at all. People that come here to be interrogated never leave here alive. Over there are several large bins. Every night, before you clean up and prepare to be picked up, you open the furnace. Be careful; it may still be hot. And then pick up one of these long shovels and clean it out, dumping everything inside into the bin. When you're done, roll the bin over there to that wall, by that elevator. They'll take it out sometime later. Questions?"

"No, Sir."

"Then, when you're ready to return to your cell, you take your gown off and throw it into one bin to be washed the next time you come down here. Then put on your prison uniform. Understand?"

"Yes, Sir. You know you don't have to treat me like I'm an idiot."

He turned and looked at me angrily. "You sayin' something stupid like that is exactly the reason I have to talk down to you like you are the stupid Convict that you are. Understand?"

"Yes, Sir," I said and glared at him.

"I'll act like I didn't see that look. Do it again, though, and I'll tell the boys that work down here that I have a practice dummy for them." He shook his head as he walked away from me. I followed.

"Don't come near me unless you want me to tie you out on that table in the other room," he said.

"You can if you want to, Sir. I am sorry about being forward like I was. Punish me," I said, "If that will get us back on an even keel."

"You are dumber than a cow turd, do you know that? I don't need your permission to punish you. You might just want to shut up and follow me so I can show you how to clean the rooms."

I went with him, and he showed me how to clean the rooms and where all the laundry materials were. When we did that, he said, "You know, you're your own worst enemy. I'm still furious with you. Come with me."

We walked through the torture room, and he talked about each piece of equipment and what I could expect to see when the torturers used them. "A lot of the stuff in here is designed to cause pain, but not to wound. This thing here is for them to electrocute people. See, it looks like one of those old crank phones, but like the old electric chair in your Sing Sing prison, it administers direct current. That's a lot more powerful than the same voltage in alternating current. Personally, I wouldn't want either."

He continued, "The prisoners lose control of almost all bodily functions when they are being shocked. This stuff over here is for cutting and stabbing. They love all this shit. They will create most of the mess you'll see. Care to try anything?"

"Uh…I guess I would have to if you ordered me to. But I'm not going to volunteer," I said.

He smiled at me and then sighed. "I would never expect you to do something like that if I or anyone else orders you to. You need to stop this submissive shit. It'll get you hurt or killed."

I asked, "Can I ask how you know so much about this stuff?"

He had a sorrowful look on his face as he answered, "When they first opened this place, they started to put a couple of us through training so we could step in if needed. I got as far as what they called the classroom exercises and walked away. The Warden called me a coward and made me be the liaison to these guys as punishment, I guess. We'd have gotten some money for any work, and the Warden would have looked like a hero."

I looked at him for a second and then shrugged. "Just shows you're a better man than them, Sir. I'm glad you walked away."

He looked at me closely for a few seconds and then said, "Thanks, 32. I was going to say something smart-mouthed, but I'll simply say that means a lot coming from you. I mean it."

He moved on. "This room is where they store the cleaning supplies. They use what they call just-in-time ordering for replacement of them. When you're down to two of anything, fill out one of these forms and leave it on the table in the Gown Room. Fresh supplies will come in, and you'll find them in the furnace room by the elevator. When they do, just slot them back in the shelves here and adjust the inventory on the form. Got that?" He looked sideways at me.

"Yes, Sir."

"Good. When we were in the supply closet, I noticed that the cleaning fluids were low. Take down one box—and they're pretty heavy, so be careful—and take out three bottles to put back in the closet," he said.

I lifted the box off the shelf. It turned out that someone had already taken two bottles out of it, and so the rest of the load shifted, and the box slipped out of my hands, smashing my left pinky against the shelf frame. I howled in pain, and the box almost fell on me. The Guard stepped over and put his hand on it so that it didn't.

"Damn, these things are heavy and unbalanced. Word to the wise, when you take something out of a box, put a mark on the box to remind you, you did next time. You, okay?" he asked.

"I don't think so." I held up the pinky, and we could see that the supply box had broken it.

"Sorry about that 32."

"Not your fault," I said. I paled with pain from the crushing injury. Just like getting a finger caught in a car door, I thought through the firestorm of pain.

"In any case, I want to be the only one to punish you." We both laughed—me, a little weakly.

In response to a question from Nurse Wretched about how I broke my pinky, I responded, "Stupid move on my part. I tried lifting something one-handed I shouldn't have. If the Guard hadn't been there, things would have been a lot worse. I might have gotten knocked out."

"Well, it's set now. I know I can't tell your kind not to use your hand for a few days but try not to put too much strain on it."

"Yes, ma'am. May I ask a question?"

"Certainly."

"What did you mean by 'your kind'?" I asked.

"Convicts, Lifers, people like you arrogant, but who're dumber than stones. People who think that they may take and the rest of us have to give. Someone whose only pleasure is whacking off, which will be a little harder for a few days." She looked at my shocked face for a few seconds. "If you hadn't wanted to get an answer like this, you shouldn't have asked, Lifer. Now get out of here and back to whatever make-work they've assigned to you."

"Come on, 32. You have important work to do," said the Guard, glaring at the nurse. As we stepped out the door, he stopped and turned. "You know, I wasn't going to say anything, but you're working in the wrong place with that attitude. Keep your thoughts about 32 to yourself in the future, or you'll have me to deal with."

As we walked back to the main building and my first time cleaning the interrogation rooms, he said, "Read nothing into that, other than I'm the only person who can dish out abuse to you. Got that?"

"Yes, Sir," copying his slight grin.

"When we're alone, you can call me Lynn."

"Yes, Sir. I mean Lynn."

As we walked back down the stairs to the interrogation rooms, he said, "This is usually pretty gross. I'm assuming they assigned you to this because you can keep it together and your mouth shut."

"I don't know why they assigned me to this other than to keep punishing me. But like I said, I can keep my mouth shut," I said.

When we opened the door to the end of the hallway, we saw a man wheeling a gurney with a cover over it into the furnace room at the other end of the hallway. I rocked back on my feet, and the Guard grabbed me by my elbow. "Keep it together," he whispered. We walked down the hall toward the Gown Room, and as we did, the stink got more and more intense. Sweat, blood, excrement, and sex were all floating in the air. Nauseating. "You'll get used to the smell."

"God, I hope not. That would mean I'd lost my soul like these people," I said.

Stopping in the hall, he gave me a good, long, appraising look and smiled regretfully.

We walked into the Gown Room, and it surprised me to see two men in there. Both were big, burly sorts who looked at me with a bit of shock and even more contempt. "This the new Fish?" one of them asked. The Guard said, "Yes. A Lifer. You can call her 32."

"Thanks. Hey, Lifer, is it true that they had you dig your own grave and spend the night in it? I thought what we did down here had its kinks, but that is truly something else. What'd you do with your finger? That looks like it's got to hurt some," asked one man.

"It does, yes," I said. "I was doing something stupid, and a large box fell on my hands, breaking the pinky."

"Damn. That'll make scrubbing the floors a little hard, I bet. Anyway, it's all yours," the man said.

The third man had come in by that time, and the guard introduced me to him. They didn't share their names. I went back to my locker, stripped, hung my clothes inside, and put on my sack. When my head popped out, I looked around, and all three of the men were staring at me.

"Lucious," said one man.

"Sorry, boys, but I'm here to work, and I've another job that starts at 6 AM," I said with a smile.

I turned and walked out of the room. "I'm not sure," the Guard said, "that they know that if they'd asked, you'd have to give it up. I won't tell them."

We walked to the cleaning closet and got my supplies. They included a few different brushes, buckets, cleaning fluids, industrial sprayers for the cleaning fluids, gloves, plastic goggles, brooms, respirators, and bags for any larger pieces of garbage. All these fit into a cart that included a large garbage pail. "So, I'm a janitor now," I said gloomily.

"More like an evidence tech at a crime scene, as you'll see. I plan to stay with you for a few hours until you get a feeling for what you need to do," said the Guard.

"No need for that, Guard. I'll take it from here," said the Warden, who had slipped in unnoticed. "I'll make sure she does a good job and then that she gets back to her cell when she's done."

The Guard looked like he was about to say something, and I spoke up, "Why thanks, Warden, Sir, this is very kind of you, even though I'm sure you've got other things that you'd rather be doing."

"Agree, 32; there are other things I'd rather be doing, but this is a significant contract for us, and I want to make sure you do an outstanding job on the clean-up with this being your first time down here. After today's meeting with the media, I know you have your wits about you and a mouth to go along with it. This is what I think you Americans call 'Belts and Suspenders,' right 32?"

"Yes, Sir. I'll do a good job and am happy that you're here to guide me." I looked at the Guard, "I guess I'll see you later."

The Guard left. The Warden looked at me carefully. "Before you go in there, a couple of things: I wasn't joking when I said that this is an important contract for us. You screw it up, and I will see that you spend the rest of your brief life down here for them to practice on. Understand, Lifer?"

"Yes, Sir. The Guard has said a similar thing to me."

"He did, did he?"

"Yes, Sir. He realizes the importance of this contract to the prison," I said.

"Good. Second, you embarrassed the government and me today. Thankfully, it was among friends, so to speak, but the media people went back, and the Governor contacted me and said that he wanted you punished for your mouth. So, since you mentioned the twenty-year agreement, I went back to look at it. It says, clearly..." and he pulled a copy out of his pocket and showed me a circled section just above my signature, "that the government or I can adjust the agreement if you don't live up to the obligations or act out. You didn't today, though, among 'friends' again, and I'm going to nip that behavior in the bud by adding five years onto your sentence. Twenty-five years now. Not twenty as you had when you walked into that meeting today. That's what you get, smart-ass. Punishment needs to be fast and severe to get the attention of douchebags like you. Now, open the door and get to work."

I didn't think my spirits could sink and further, but they did. I also knew much more was to come this evening. I opened the door to the room and nearly threw up. There was blood, other liquids, and tissue everywhere. Stepping into the room, I almost and would have fallen if the Warden hadn't caught me. "Gotta remember to get sandals with better treads on them for you. Those sandals you have aren't worth a shit."

"Thank you for catching me, Warden."

"You're welcome, 32. By the way, do you have any pet names you'd like me to call you? If you don't, I'll come up with one."

"I can't think of one, Sir."

"Well, how about Muff? I like that. It means what you are. Put on the respirator. Otherwise, you'll be smelling this for days."

"Now, the best way to clean these rooms is from the top down. That way, anything that runs down runs over places you haven't cleaned yet. Open the sprayer's top and follow the instructions on that industrial cleaner over there. These things are caustic, so make sure you wear your gloves. We wouldn't want your hands to lose that nice, soft skin, would we?"

"No, Sir. Thank you, Sir."

"Here, let me help you get the glove on over that splint. How could you be so clumsy? This will hurt." And it did.

He showed me how to spray down the room, starting at the ceiling and working down. The power sprayer helped a lot. Once the walls and flat surfaces were all cleaned, he told me to get a bucket full of water, get on my hands and knees and scrub the floor clean of the remaining blood and any debris. When I'd done that, about an hour and a half into the night's work, he told me to scoop up the rubbish and to put it into a bag.

"Good job. You'll get better and faster at it, Muff, with time. The next thing you need to do is take the polishing machine here once the floor dries and finish the job. Everything needs to sparkle. In the meantime, I see that the floor out here in the hallway is messy as well. I want you to fill a bucket with boiling water and more of the cleaner and get down on your hands and knees and clean this up as well."

The hallway was about 60 feet long, so this took another hour and a half, and he stood there watching my bare rear the whole time. It was now a little after 2:30 AM. I saw some movement down the hall at the doorway to the furnace room. The red light in the ceiling there had turned to green.

"Warden, what does it mean when that red light turns to green down there?"

"That means that the cremation cycle is completed. When that green light turns off, maybe in a half hour or so, you should be able to go in there and clean out the furnace. I won't go in there with you for that. You'll see why. We probably have a half hour before you'll be able to run the polisher. Let's go check out the rest area and grab something to eat and talk some more or do something else." He looked at me with a smile that I didn't like and filled with clear intent.

We found a well-stocked kitchen in the rest area. He pulled a few things out and told me to make us something to eat. I did, and he sat and observed me, showing particular interest when I had to stretch to grab things off higher shelves.

"Do you like freeze-dried soups, Muff? I know I should have asked."

"It's been a long time, Sir, but yes."

"Yeah, I suppose that was a dumb question. You've been here, what, 11 months? That would make you almost 22, right? Do you ever think of what you're missing out there? After what your supposed friends said about you, I wouldn't miss them for sure," the Warden said.

"May I sit, Sir?"

"Not right away. Stand right there. Answer my questions."

"I was in law school, Sir. That's behind me now, for sure. I'm just focused on making it day by day, Sir. I'll do what I need to do to survive and maybe get out of here someday. I think every day about what I am missing on the outside. I've no access to news or anything so that the world could've blown up, and I wouldn't know," I said.

"You're right about maybe not getting out of here. You keep mouthing off like you did today, you'll do Life Plus. Do you know what that is?"

"No, Sir, though I've heard some people talking about it."

"Well, Life Plusers are people who have a sentence of life plus some number of years or consecutive life terms. You don't see them around here because they're kept in a separate compound out there." And he gestured out toward the swamp. "I'll see that you spend a few weeks or months out there to get a taste of what that life is like. In one way of thinking about it, you're already a Life Pluser if you take the deal off the table. It might be an education for you. What do you say about that?" he asked.

"I'm not sure what you want me to say, Sir. This place is already Hell. Could this new place be worse?"

"Well, you've had a few years of college under your belt. Ever hear of Dante Alighieri?"

"Yes, Sir." I knew keeping him talking might delay him from whatever else he had planned for me.

"Well, if you know Dante and you know his Nine Circles of Hell? Well, this is only a little different. The prison you were in is, say, the First Circle, Limbo. You're maybe in the Fourth Circle right now, Greed. If you think of it, that's what got you in trouble in the first place. You can look at the Life Plus camp being in the lower reaches of Hell. I'm not sure, but well below the ninth circle," he said.

"Finish your soup," he said. "You know, something else needs to happen to you as payback for embarrassing me today. I've got them right here." He produced a set of thumb cuffs. "We'll try these out soon." I sighed audibly, and he smiled sadistically at me.

I worked with the polisher. That took another hour, and when I looked at the digital clock at the end of the hallway, I realized I'd not get to *my* bed that night.

"You've done a good job here, Muff. You should be proud of that, but pride got yourself in here in the first place, so be careful. Now, the furnace room. That's on your own," said the Warden.

I walked down the hall to the room. The warning light had been off for some time, so I thought the furnace would have cooled. I was very wrong. I opened the furnace door and was hit immediately with a blast of super-hot air. I felt my skin burn and left the door ajar for another half hour for the crematorium to cool enough to access it. The Warden had disappeared into the rest area, so I felt safe just standing in the hallway.

Finally, I braced myself and walked into the furnace room. I started sweating right away. Sliding the tools and ash bin over to the furnace door, I put on a pair of asbestos gloves and an apron that hung next to the door. When I opened the furnace door completely, another blast of heat hit me, as well as the cooked body's stink.

I stuck the shovel in and began filling the bin with the ash. It wasn't long before I hit something substantial. I pulled it out; it was what I thought might be a leg bone, and I gagged. After sucking in a breath of the hot, putrid air, the loading of the bin continued. Several more times, I hit bones and once or twice a piece of fused jewelry, those I put aside. Far in the back of the furnace, near the gas jets, I saw something lodged between the jets and the furnace's back wall. It took some work, but it came out and rolled toward me—a skull. I fell backward and hit the floor hard, and the skull rolled out and landed in my lap. It was scorching and burned my thighs a bright red. I pushed it off and put it into the bin with the rest of the ash and bones.

"So, how was that 32? Enjoy that first experience? You'll get it at least once a week from now on," said the Warden.

The laundry was the last thing to be done. I returned to the lockers, collected the laundry, and brought it back to the laundry room, where I started the two washers.

"Why don't you just toss your smock into the machine as well?" said the Warden. "Then we can have a little R&R while the machines work."

I saw no way out of what was coming, "Yes, Sir," and I pulled the smock off and started the machine. He walked over and set the wash cycle for an hour and hit the start button.

"Come on, Muff. I want to try out yours," he said with a laugh and waved the cuffs at me.

It was a long hour and a painful one. He took off the cuffs when it was over and told me to run into the laundry room and move the clothes over to the dryers. "Set those to 90 minutes, Muff, so that I can have some more fun."

Just spectacular, I thought.

"By the way, you've been here long enough to have a day off. Let's make it today," said the Warden.

"Yes, Sir," I said, resigned to this fate.

When the drying cycle ended, I took out the clothes, folded some, and set aside the clothes that needed to be ironed. I put the clothes in the correct lockers, including my potato sack when I did all of that.

The Warden was lying on the bed, naked, when I walked back into the sleeping room. He patted the bed next to him and asked, "You done?"

"Yes, Sir."

"Good. Come here and snuggle and let's get some sleep," he said.

Funny, but that is what we did. I felt, for a moment anyway, that I was being treated a little less the whore. I knew that wouldn't last long.

He had his left arm wrapped around my chest with his fingers on my nipple. He'd played with it a lot the previous night, and I found I liked the combination of pain and pleasure he gave. I could see his watch and noted the date and time. I'd been entirely wrong about the date. I thought it was much later and frowned; my life here was passing far more slowly than I'd thought. Discomfort slows things down, I thought.

Toward morning, I slipped out from underneath the Warden's arm to go to the bathroom, closing the door quietly. Midway through my movement, the door opened, and the Warden stood there looking down on me. "Do you get any privacy like this in prison, Convict?"

"No, Sir; no doors to close."

He turned to walk away, leaving the door open, and as he did, he said, "See that you remember that in the future."

When I finished, I walked out into the room. He was dressing. "Put these sheets into the laundry and give them a good wash. I'm going back to my quarters to wash your stink off."

Well, back to normal, I thought.

| 4 |

Tropical Storm Desiree

The Next 9 Months; Time Flies (It Does):

Time lumbered on—nothing new day after day. There was nothing to look forward to except working out and sparring with Paola—and, perversely, spending time with the Warden. Cycles of boredom, painful, interminable boredom, interspersed with moments of horror and terror, almost like someone once said about war, but without the goals of peace and freedom.

My relationships with Paola and the Guard continued to deepen. Precisely what I had read prison was about. I frequently thought about standards and how mine had changed over time, in many different directions, not what I would have ever believed, but several still exciting as several more were, well, not.

Tropical Storm Desiree was forecasted to be worse than Tropical Super Storm Sandy in 2012. When it hit the Island, sustained winds were greater than 35 miles per hour, and the storm-battered the Islands; it went back out into the Caribbean and then came back in again, each time dumping over 15 inches of rain. The storm destroyed almost all roads and critical infrastructure. The rinse and repeat cycle it used was like Tropical Storm Allison that had battered Houston in 2001.

Shepherd Island flooded because of the 15-foot storm surge, and all the prisoners lived on the second floors of the prisons until they could take us out on airboats for work details. We couldn't go back to the prison for a very long time after they evacuated us.

They put me on a work detail assigned to clearing Island roads to get rescue vehicles through. We Convicts couldn't use chain saws, axes, and saws, because they couldn't trust us with weapons, they said. More likely, it was because they didn't want the population to see murderers and the worst of society doing anything but laboring like slaves along the side of the roads. But we could dig and carry, which we did for months, finally returning the Island to a semblance of normalcy. My favorite jobs were throwing debris into the big chippers the U.S. FEMA brought in for breakup of limbs and other things and the walk-behind trencher machine that reminded me of the plows I'd pulled before I became a Lifer. It was the only machine they'd let us use because it wouldn't make a suitable weapon—as if we would have used any of the things they could have issued us as weapons. Where the hell would we have gone if we broke out?

Of course, the first place we worked was on the part of the Island where the high-end hotels were. That most of the population was stranded and without access to food and clean water didn't seem to matter. Getting the hotels back online did. The storm utterly wrecked most of these places. I'd seen pictures of the Gulf Coast hotels after Rita, with hotel and casino windows all blown out and curtains hanging out of them. These were like that. But because building standards here were very different from the U.S., many of the hotels were significantly impacted structurally by the storm. It might be years before some of them got back into operation. Many would have to be rebuilt entirely from the ground up.

Our work on the hotels began on the top floors of them. Usually, before engineers got in there to say that the building was safe, we were in there tearing out everything to the cinderblock walls. It was fun throwing stuff out of 10th-floor windows and watching it crash to the ground below. That is until I got assigned to one of the work crews clearing that debris on the ground.

We slept in the hotels at night, chained together, as if, again, we had somewhere to go. I even got to see my old hotel room. I asked to be assigned to demolish it, and the Guard and I did. I surprised him with my enjoyment in smashing the place. He laughed with me when I told him why.

The work was backbreaking and never seemed to end. We prisoners would finish moving or clearing one area, and then we'd be transported to another to work, more accurately, slave. I wore the same clothes for months as the storm destroyed the prison's uniform center. The Guard told me to be prepared to wear it for a heck of a lot longer. He worked side-by-side with me, as did the other Lifer Guards. They pulled their weight. I was and wasn't surprised. These guys were devoted to their work and partners, almost like a marriage, but without the rings.

When we slept outside the hotels, something that didn't happen for days at a stretch, we did as a group in a ditch or chained to trees. But for the bugs, this was pretty nice. I also liked that I got a chance to meet several of the Lifer Pluses that the Warden and I had talked about. The girls I spoke to told me they were working on an important project away from the central prison. Desiree wiped out most of their work, and they had to look forward to rebuilding their Camp and rebooting that work. Maybe next time, they told me, they'd be further along with it, and the damage here from something like Desiree would be a lot less. That intrigued me, but we didn't have a whole lot of time to talk.

Paola and I worked shoulder during this time as well, pacing and challenging each other. Both our Guards told us to lighten up because they couldn't keep up with us. We told them to stop whining, catch up or shut up. We all had a lot of friendly laughs at each other's expenses.

One, probably the only, good thing about the storm—and it indeed wasn't good for anyone—was that it was a break in the mind-numbing routine we all usually suffered. When I returned to the prison, I found that the people left behind had done little to prepare for our return. So, we had to turn to making our homes as livable as we could again. That took several months as there was no money to buy anything we needed to return the prison to its former barbaric glory. We made do, though, and made the place better.

When life returned to more or less normal, the Lifer Guards had another task for the Lifers. We all had to re-dig our graves that the storm had flooded and washed away. This time, though, they didn't make us spend the night in them. I guess a kind of recognition and reward for our hard work over the last months. I also got to tap in four more "32" labeled markers. I was pretty sure they were nowhere near the graves of those poor souls.

I had one more task: Desiree had flooded the basement interrogation center and destroyed almost everything down there. I worked hard to get it returned to operation, not that I wanted that to happen at all. The Warden forced the Guard and me to work with the interrogators to pump the place out and clean it up. Well, that was a task for a Lifer. The interrogators weren't there for most of that work, and when they were, they acted like prima donnas ordering us around. The Guard protested to the Warden but was told to keep his mouth shut and do their work.

When I say "destroyed," I genuinely meant that. All the equipment they had was ruined and had to be replaced. Crates of it came in, and they tasked me with reassembling it. One interrogator handled the lights and electrical stuff, but I got the rest, including the crematorium. There, I got to climb into what they called the retort or the crematorium chamber and scrub it out and clean all the burners—a miserable job. I got covered with filth and frequently cut my hands on the burner flanges that had gotten rusty after the flooding. Thankfully, they let me use the showers down there to clean up after every session.

When we fixed everything, they let me press the button to start the burners and watch it go through a cycle or two. They made me stay in the room for the entire process, as they wanted nothing to go wrong and to cause a fire or an explosion. I would have been happy with that if I wasn't in the room the entire time. I was little better than fresh fish for them.

Reassembling their torture devices was less fun because the instructions came with videos and instruction manuals that set out how users used them. I'd not seen any of that, being clean up, but now I saw the many ways that trained torturers used these things, and it repulsed me even more, just like it had Lynn. One guy was working on the lights when I put one X-frame together. He taught me all about how they used it. For some reason, he thought I was interested. I listened politely, though, as I was sure these were people you didn't piss off.

"This thing used to be called the St. Andrew's Cross. They used it in the Middle Ages as a torture device. BDSM-types here use it in their cellars. It makes a great whipping post. Want me to try you out on it?" he asked.

"Uh. No thanks. Maybe some other time. I have a lot of other things I need to do down here." I was pretty sure he was serious.

| 5 |

Two Years in Purgatory and then the Ninth Circle

The Next 24 Months; Time Slows, Again:

Schopenhauer said, "The two enemies of happiness are pain and boredom." He had that right. The following days and months, twenty-four of them, settled back into the same boring, painful routine. I worked outside, inside, janitorial services in the interrogation area, and my weekly liaison with the Warden. He seemed to get great pleasure out of those times, and the more he did, the less I did.

My other least favorite thing was seeing the media people. The group leader, Francis "Frankie" Geap, seemed to love causing me embarrassment and pain. So, the more nude filming, the better. She even talked the Warden into letting her cameraman and her film in the interrogation area. They used the shots of me on my hands and knees, scrubbing the floors a lot.

Then came the day for the joint interview with the family of the deceased. It was as horrific as I thought it would be. From the beginning, the family called me vile things I probably deserved, but not to be said in front of international media. Frankie shot three interviews with the family and then spent hours with the Warden and me watching the last takes. All made a case for me being a monstrous, unredeemable evil.

"I'm pleased with these, 32; I want you also to do a series with the families of the people who were quarantined and maybe some street interviews. How'd you like that?" asked Frankie.

"Does it matter what I say, Frankie? You're going to do what you want, anyway. Please, torment me as much as you want, you sadistic bitch," I said.

Frankie looked blankly at me. The Warden glowered. The Guard rolled his eyes.

"I want to see you in my office in three hours, 32. You're going to the Justus Angel and Mistress L. Horry Camp for that month, I promised you a while ago. Does that surprise you? You thought that since I made nice to you a few times, there might be something here like, maybe, respect for you. No way. Not going to happen. Ever. Three hours to say your good-byes."

Three hours later, the Guard and I were at the Warden's office. He made us sit outside of it for another hour, and then we were told we could go in. There were two men there with the Warden.

"Guard, I think you know these men," said the Warden.

"Yes, Sir. It's good to see you both again. It's been a long time," he said with a smile and shook both their hands. The relationships seemed warm, and I assumed this might not be too bad for me. Once again, my biases were to bite me.

"It has. We're isolated out there at the Camp, but it sure isn't boring. We've got a wonderful project going that this one will fit right into. We've been having all these floods because the barrier islands are being washed away by the seas' rise, especially after Desiree, which set us back. Well, we're building them back up. Tough, strong convicts like this one will be extremely helpful, even if it's only for two years."

I looked up, shocked. "Yes, 32, two years. I might have said something shorter, but these men convinced me that anything shorter would be inconvenient for them and not give you a full flavor for the Camp you could well end up in forever. The good news for you is that the Guard here has volunteered to accompany you. The bad news is that the media folks want to come and film you to show how far you've fallen. Don't worry, though. We put a temp in downstairs, and you'll have your old job as soon as you're back here. I understand the boys down there are planning to ramp up the operation, so you might just get to live down there permanently. Now, you, 32, get out of here so I can talk to these men," the Warden said, dismissing me back to the hallway where I was made to stand to wait for them.

They put the obligatory belt and arm and ankle cuffs on me when they did but didn't shackle me. They gave me a pair of sandals to wear, telling me it was a long hike to the Camp. They also warned me about running off because the swamp was full of sinkholes and unfriendly creatures.

Justus Angel and Mistress L. Horry were notorious Black slave owners in South Carolina in the 1830s. They treated their slaves as less than property, so selecting that name for this Camp was not a little intended to convey a message to the inmates. Angel and Horry were not well-liked by their slaves, and they treated them harshly if they didn't work hard or tried to escape. The Lifer Pluses here didn't like their administrators as well. I was going to find out why, but then to make a friend unexpectedly.

It was a three-day walk to the Camp through the swamp. Because they cuffed my hands to my waist, the bugs would have eaten me alive except for the lemon eucalyptus oil that my Guard kept smearing on my face and exposed body parts. It had the added benefit of smelling good as well. Better than I had smelled for quite a while, anyway.

I carried all the supplies we'd need for the day trips. Like a pack animal, I had a heavy backpack on my front and back. I was strong, but the substantial extra weight made me unbalanced, so I fell several times. The Guard led me on the end of a leash, and he pulled me hard when I flagged. "You hold us up from reaching the first cache before dark, and they'll have to whip you. Move, 32." Later he told me he was sorry for the way he spoke to me but was afraid that the Warden would re-assign him if it looked like we were too friendly. I told him I wasn't looking for any favors but thanked him.

Parts of the walk were through shallow water that surrounded hummocks. One of the Assistant Wardens showed me how dangerous the swamps were. "See that hummock over there, Convict?"

"Yes, Sir."

"Watch," and he threw a large stick at it. When it hit, the hill erupted into motion. A giant alligator thrashed around and then dove into the water. "Why you need to stick with us. Understand, Convict?" By the end of our hike, the Guard had taught me how to distinguish real hummocks from the alligator homes. That would be helpful knowledge later.

"Yes, Sir." I'd become resigned to being treated like a dumb pack animal but appreciated the instruction.

After a few more hours of walking, we reached the thing the Guard had called a cache. It was a sealed metal box that contained tents, food, water, camp stoves, and pots. They released me from my cuffs and told me to prepare them their dinners. "Three servings," said one of the Assistant Wardens. "You get fed later if you show you're worth it."

I worked hard and fast to prepare them their meals. When they sat down to eat them in front of me, one Assistant Warden told me to kneel. The other walked behind me, grabbed my arms, and pinioned them to the back of the belt. He then dropped a line from the end of the belt to my ankle cuffs and bound my ankle cuffs to my waist. He then kicked me over on my side, basically hog-tied. Why are they doing this, I asked myself? I looked plaintively at the Guard, who could only shrug.

They ate their meals and talked about the years they'd spent together in the military and how they missed them. Now and then, one of them threw a chunk of meat or something toward me and told me to squirm over to get it. As a result, I was coated with filth and soaked to the skin. The Guard let them know that he thought this was wrong and walked over and fed me a few pieces of meat from his meal. The Assistants chided him about being a wimp.

When they finished, one Assistant said, "Time for a little fun. Want something in your stomach, Convict?"

Weakly, I said, "Yes, Sir," knowing what was coming, no pun intended.

They pulled me up on my knees and started in on me. The Guard said this was even further beyond the pale, and he wouldn't take part. They laughed at him and called him a sucker. After they were done with me, the Guard rolled me in a blanket and then tied a rope around it, so I was completely immobilized. "Best I can do for you. Sorry, you don't get a tent," he said.

The following day, they woke me early and let me go off into the trees with the Guard to pee. I did. He then helped me get dressed. "I know it's going to hurt given last night, but you have to keep the pace up today. If you don't and we're late getting to the next cache, they'll whip you, and there'll be nothing I can do about it."

"I understand...," I looked around and saw the two men were far away on the other side of the campsite and ducked my head toward the Guard, "Lynn." He smiled at me.

"You're a riddle to me, 32."

The day's walk was like the previous, but out in more sun. I felt like I was burning up. We stopped three times, not for me, because they made me stand when they stopped, but for them to rest. We reached the second cache before sunset. Everyone was exhausted, but not so much that they would let me rest. The night was a repeat of the previous one.

The walk on the third day was shorter than the first two, but we had to walk through some deep water. Before we entered it, the men took three wet suits and wet suit booties out of the packs. I breathed easier because that considerably reduced the weight I was carrying. Little did I know the reason they needed the suits.

Our next landfall was about a mile away, one of the Assistants told me. We entered the water and started wading across a shallow lake. The water was about chest high on me. When we climbed out of it, the Assistants turned around, looked at me, and laughed. I looked at what they were laughing at and saw dozens of leeches on my body. I gagged.

"One thing's for sure until you see the vet at the Camp, I'm not doing anything more with you, 32," said one Assistant.

We walked on and then across about another mile of water. Whether or not they were there, I felt the leeches crawling up inside of me. The thought disgusted me.

The Camp was just on the other side of this last lake. It looked like something I once saw in a picture of a North Vietnamese encampment. There were a couple of houses and then several thatched huts. Not unlike the Vietnam prison pictures I'd seen, there were several grates set into the ground. I could only imagine what those were for. I didn't realize I'd be getting up close and personal with one of them pretty soon.

We walked into the Camp, and they took me to the infirmary and a real "Doctor." He poked and prodded me and removed the leeches, saying he didn't think he saw any when he looked up into my vagina and ass. "But I could just as easily be wrong," he said. "If you feel sick in the next few days, let me know."

When we came out of the infirmary building, I was unsurprised to see the media team there. They'd set up some cameras and interviewed the Assistant Wardens, my Guard, and several prisoners about life at the Justus Angel and Mistress L. Horry Camp.

"Wonderful. Now, can you tell me what 32 here can expect to experience while she's here?" Frankie turned to me and said with a sadistic grin, "I've explained to them who you are, and they're interested in why you did what you did. I'm sure they're going to give you a lot of opportunities to explain yourself."

They spent the rest of the day filming the group working on the barrier islands project. One of the older women explained they'd been at the project for nearly two years and had been seeing some impacts of their work on the erosion until Desiree. It was grueling work, she said, but with it, this group of people who took much could give back. She was under two consecutive life sentences and thirty years. Aside from me, the only person with less than multiple successive life sentences was another woman sentenced to life plus 15 years, like what the courts had threatened me with. She was the Lifer Plus I'd talked to when we were doing the Desiree work.

All the women sported the same numbered brands, as I did with one addition. They branded them on their hip and breast with an "L+" to show their status. They took me off for that as well.

"Don't worry, 32. When we get back, I'll have that branded over, but while you're here, you need to be one of the girls," said the Guard.

The blacksmith here was one of the Assistant Wardens. He told me to strip. I did, and they took my clothes away and put them in a fire. As before, the media crew used the opportunity of my nudity to paw and maltreat me. I took it stoically, realizing part of the reason I was there was because I had mouthed off to these people. The Guard stood by and watched, clearly upset for me. Later, I saw him in an animated conversation with Frankie, who seemed to come out on the short end of whatever they were talking about. Years later, I would find out what he'd said to her.

When I eventually went into the blacksmith's hut, I saw they'd set it up with cameras and lights. The blacksmith told me to spread myself out on the anvil chest up. Frankie ordered, "The last time, 32, they did this to you, the blacksmith at the prison told me you barely reacted. This time I want you to wail and cry. Make a scene. Fight a bit."

"Can I use the crop on her then?" asked the Assistant.

"Would you normally if someone acted out?"

"Of course," he said.

"Then I'd say you do nothing different. Everything depends on you, 32. Give a show, and I'll make sure that this whipping is all you'll experience here," said Frankie. I wanted to strangle her.

"Vicious bitch," I thought but decided I needed to play along.

"I'm very good at what I do, 32. This will hurt a lot, so screaming doesn't have to be an act," said the Assistant.

They tied ropes around my hands and feet, and the Assistant reached into the fire and pulled out a bright red iron. He immediately swung around and drove it into my chest, just above the other brands. I screamed and cried and wasn't play-acting. But there was little I could do because of the ropes. This brand went down at least half an inch into my breast tissue.

They untied me and then told me to roll over, so my butt was up. I rolled and kept going so that I was on my feet. I heard the whiz in the air of the crop, ducked, and, when the Assistant was off-balance, kicked out, not to injure him but to take him out of the fight. I reached down and picked up the crop and lashed out at one of the other staff who had tried to sneak up on me. Someone ran into me, and I whirled to find Frankie.

I raised my arm to give the bitch a good shot in the face, heard a loud crack, and then felt a burning sensation across my back, belly, and breasts. I turned to see the other Assistant with a bullwhip. He raised it again, and I raised my hands in surrender.

"Finish with her and then bring her out here," he ordered.

They tied me out again and applied the brand to my ass. It hurt like hell, as did the one on my chest, but the fight invigorated me. They led me outside. Two of the men had raised a metal frame with leather straps at each of the corners. I fought, but there was no way I was going to win. They tied me out spread eagle on the frame. The Assistant said, "25 strokes on her tits and ass, 50 on her back, and then 20 on her belly. Then one month in the hole."

"I'll take this," said the other Assistant, the one I'd attacked.

When the Assistant finished the 90 strokes, I was a bloody mess. The media people got more and better footage than they'd expected. This would help them with the incorrigibility message they were also developing, Frankie told me. I almost passed out several times, but they weren't about to let me have that release from the punishment. Each time I passed out, they woke me up and then continued the whipping.

In the infirmary, the doctor layered medicines and compresses on my back and front. He also made a successful case to the Assistants that I should rest and heal a few days before putting me in the hole where I would only get an infection if the wounds hadn't knitted. The Guard stayed with me. When no one was watching, he held my hand. I was barely conscious but felt his kindness. I wondered what had changed with him. I would have to ask him.

Four days later, I walked out of the infirmary and straight into the hole where they threw me without ceremony. The media folks captured everything on video.

"Reach up, Convict, and lock these cuffs onto that bracket up there. If I gotta come down there, you won't like it," said the Assistant Warden I'd attacked. Still pissed off at me, I guess. I smiled inside.

I reached up, grabbed the bar, grabbed one cuff and closed it on my wrist, and then did the same with the other. I hung down with my toes, barely touching the ground at the bottom of the hole.

"Turn off the pump," the Assistant Warden ordered.

I heard a pump shut off, and the Assistant looked said to me, "Watch down there." Water seeped into the hole. "The water table is about 6 inches below the brackets. You'll be fed once a day. It's a liquid diet, we call it sludge, and we'll pour it through a pipe that'll be lowered into the hole. When I close this top, you won't see anyone or the sun for a month. Of course, you'll feel it." The cover slammed down, and I was in semi-darkness. In minutes, the hole heated up.

Over the next month, I gradually lost all sense of feeling and who I was. What I was experiencing now explained the lost looks on some women Lifer's faces. A month down here would be like the ninth circle of Dante's Inferno that the Warden had talked about. And it was.

I hallucinated a lot. The sludge I expected to be some toxic brew designed to make me sick. Instead, it was cool relative to the oven in which I was parboiling and tasted like a smoothy. I imagined it was chock full of stuff to keep me marginally healthy. It also contained, I was to find out, significant doses of anabolic steroids because they wanted to build up my strength and see other changes. This was on the Warden's orders.

One of the most frequent hallucinations was of me with Hector and Esmeralda. I was tearing them limb from limb and screaming like a beast. It made me feel good in some ways but scared me in most others. Little did I know this was likely a side-effect of me habituating to the steroids, and my screams were real. I also dreamed a lot of Paola. And about what things might be like with the Guard. My fantasies helped me get through the month.

I also lost all decency, the last vestiges of civilization. They had taken almost all of it out of me when we displayed all body functions all the time. I was fine now with peeing and pooping right where I hung; I had no choice. The other thing about the hole was that I was sure that I wasn't alone. Though I was sure there were no rats in the hole with me, I felt things crawling on my body. I gave up caring about that too, eventually, thinking it was another hallucination. Most likely was.

One day, the grate opened, and the Guard looked down at me. "How are you, 32?" he asked.

"Just fine, Guard, just fine. I loved the month on the beach. Could you get me out of here?" I replied, feeling fuzzy.

He smiled and said, "Sure." He climbed down into the hole and released my cuffs. He caught me as I slid under the water. "Got you."

"I can't use my arms," I said.

"It'll be okay. You'll get feeling back in a few minutes. And you won't like it." He was right. As the feeling returned, my arms burned, and my muscles spasmed. I whimpered. "Your legs may need some retraining, but I'm here for you," he whispered into my ear.

The feeling returned over the next several days, starting with intense burning in my arm and leg muscles. I was very unsteady on my feet. With help, I started moving around. The Guard rubbed my muscles, and with some homeopathic cures and exercise, I gradually built back strength. "I'm surprised that you didn't suffer more. Your muscle mass looks damn good."

"I'd hope so," one of the Assistant Wardens said. "We've been dosing her with anabolic steroids. How are you feeling, honey?"

During my rehab, I learned that the month I was in the hole was the longest of the women. And since I didn't come out like a babbling lunatic, I was viewed by Guards and Convicts alike like a superstar. The second-longest was a woman who'd been buried in the prison graveyard the day we had left to walk out to the Camp.

They handcuffed me to the hospital bed all the time I was there as if I could go anywhere on my own power. What that meant, though, was someone had to be around all the time to help me, initially with bedpans and then eventually so I could go to the bathroom. The task fell to the Guard, though the doctor would spell him several times a day.

One night, I woke up to see him sitting a few feet from the bed, reading. He had a light covered so it wouldn't disturb me. I smiled and thought that was so sweet. As I did, I fell back asleep and recalled that I needed to talk to him about what had changed.

A few days later, when the two of us had taken a long walk around the periphery of the Camp, and I came back not winded, I asked, "Guard, is there anything that I could ever do to repay your friendship?"

He looked at me and smiled. "Stop being stupid, maybe? I don't want to see you getting hurt anymore. You're your own worst enemy. Maybe a little one-in-one time, too."

"You mean one-*on*-one?"

"I said what I meant. I haven't done that with you because I think all of this is so abusive. If I had my way, all of it would end. Maybe this place too, at least in the way it's being run now," he said.

"Later, gator on the one-in-one time; I'm down with that," I said with a smile. "Another question: What's changed with you? I saw it after we did the walk from the prison to here. I think you care for me."

"I hope I'm not that obvious to everyone else," he said, looking around a little. "I do care for you, 32, and I also see more and more how cruel we are here. You've been right in some things you've said to me and others. I'm going to see if there is more I can do for you and the other women. You're paying for your crimes, and we should make sure that is all that happens. You did wrong and are here to do time for it. The suffering, besides that, that the Warden permits, no encourages, is depraved... Besides, I'm taken with you. Scruffy as you are, you're smart and powerful. Not just physical strength, though there is surely that. Mental and moral strength that I didn't expect to see in you given what you did to get yourself in here. If we can do it and not get ourselves in trouble, I want to learn more about you."

We started on that later that night when everyone was asleep. I thought I might be falling in love. I knew I shouldn't do this—fall in love—but I thought back to my lovemaking with Hector and concluded that it didn't come close to this in terms of intensity of feelings. Maybe that was because of all that I'd been through, but maybe there was something to this man. Since the stint in the hole and my rehab, I had taken to calling him "my" Guard publicly. He didn't dissuade me, though he asked me to tone it down in front of the Wardens, Assistants, and guards.

I wanted to get out to the project, but they said I'd have to wait another month. Instead, I was put to work in the kitchen, as a janitor, and in the laundry. All jobs I had plenty of practice doing. At the end of a month, I felt sound enough to get out with the general population.

My Guard still took me out for walks, then runs, and then worked out to rebuild my lost coordination. One Assistant, the one who'd beaten me, watched me work out one day and asked me if I ever did martial arts. "Yes, a little MMA here in prison."

"You move like you do. Want to spar?" he asked.

"I'm not sure I'm ready for that," I said.

"You'll never know if you don't try. Come over here," he replied.

He led me over to the ring. "Before we go in, am I just to be a punching bag, or can I fight too?" I asked. I added, "I can do either, Sir."

He smiled mock evilly, "If you don't fight, then I'm putting you back in the hole for three months."

"Okay, then."

The more we fought, the more my muscle memory returned, and I saw how this man was sloppy. The first day, he beat me soundly three times, even bloodying my nose. The second day was more of the same. On the third day, he launched himself into a roundhouse kick during the last match, and I dodged it, sending him to the ground, bruising his shin. I beat him that day one match, and then over the following days, we broke roughly even.

After the second week of that, he said, "Time for you to go out to the project, Convict. Thanks for playing with me, and you could've been quite good if you hadn't taken this turn."

"Sir, can I ask you a question?"

My Guard's head shot up. This never ended well.

"Okay, sure."

"Why do you guys always do this? You should give credit where it's due but not follow it with something that diminishes and degrades us, Convicts. Now, for most of these women, me included maybe, we're going nowhere except back to a grave like the one I have waiting for me. That makes it even more important to make us feel some self-worth," I said.

"Huh... Convict, I ought to send you back into the hole, except for one thing; you're right—one more round. I won't hold back, and I expect you not to either," he said.

It was a vicious fight. We bloodied and bruised each other until we called it a draw. I was glad we'd called it quits because he'd hit me in the eye, and it was impacting my depth perception. He was happy because he was concerned that one of my roundhouse kicks might have aggravated an old Achilles Tendon injury.

"Damn good fight, Lifer. Remind me to have you at my back for a fight."

"Thank you, Sir. I feel the same, even if we got off on the wrong foot."

| 6 |

There Are Real Pirates in the Caribbean?

Still Inside the 24 months:

The next day, while sore, I could walk to the barrier islands project, about a mile away. Several nature conservancies and the State jointly supported the project, with the State's contribution being the conscripted labor. They set poles into the sea bottom about a hundred yards out every hundred feet or so, announcing the project and that this was a no-trespass zone.

Half of the prisoners were working on the project at any time. The other half was back at the Camp, arguably resting. Each tour at the project was five days, and we worked from dawn until dark, moving earth dredged up and dropped on the shore to use to rebuild the islands; so upwards of thirteen hours a day. Eventually, there were to be five islands, but at that point, we had completed one and started on the second that Desiree had severely damaged. The prisoners worked, ate, and slept on the islands we were building. When we arrived, the first thing we did at each site was to make our prison enclosure, which generally comprised a series of poles to which chains were attached and then attached at night to our ankle cuffs. The Assistants told us that if there were a storm, the guards would try to reach us to free us so we could all survive. They emphasized the word "try."

"Wow. This looks like it is going to be fun," I said.

"If you're into brutal labor under the relentless sun, I'd agree," said my Guard.

I immediately joined in and, for the next three days, threw myself into the job. Each night I was exhausted and slept well under the stars. And each day, I felt stronger. I asked my Guard and the Assistant if I could do a consecutive five-day rotation. They looked at each other, and then the Assistant said there was nothing sacred about five days. So, they agreed—ten days here and then five days back at the Camp for me. I loved the exposure to the elements and the work.

I'd been through five cycles of project work and "rest," so two-and-a-half months had almost passed, and I felt better than expected, so much so, I was tempted to ask to stay after the two years were over. I wasn't sure what that would mean, but I liked the idea. I wouldn't want to lose my Guard, though.

We had just started eating breakfast on our second day of this cycle when a ship appeared offshore. A dinghy manned by, we could see, four men came toward us from the boat. My favorite Assistant Warden "friend" walked down to the beach to warn them away. When they neared the shore, he said something to the men, and one of them produced a gun and shot him down.

"Shit," said my Guard. "Everyone over here." He began removing the leg cuffs. The other guards helped as well. They sent the women into the water to swim to the shore and hide in the jungle as they finished.

I stayed to help my Guard and the others. The four armed men walked toward us just as we released the last prisoner, who swam away.

"Stop there, or we'll shoot." Two of the men had AKs and pointed them in our direction.

I looked at the ship and saw two more dinghies heading toward us. "We need to get out of here," I said to the group. "I'll distract them. As soon as I do, make a run for it."

"No, you won't," said my Guard.

I stepped toward the men with my hands up. I walked about 10 yards toward them and kneeled, clasping my hands behind my head. I smiled and said to my Guard, "This is why I'm here, and they shot my friend. Payback time."

"Look at this one, Enrique. Pretty hot, ain't she?" said one man, the man, I think, who'd shot my friend.

"Yeah, and I think I recognize her. What's your name, Convict?" asked the one called Enrique.

"Claire, Sir. Claire McGinnis."

The man smiled and turned to his friends. "Well, boys. This one is a celebrity. Remember that American Puta supposed student that violated quarantine regulations here? Well, this is her. I heard one person she infected with the disease died, and so she's now a Lifer."

"A Lifer Plus, Sir," I said.

"What's that, Puta?"

"My sentence is life, plus my original sentence, which was 12 years by the time the man died. So, life plus 12. I never get out of prison, in other words."

"And how does that make you feel, Puta?" Enrique asked.

"It is what it is, and now I am what I am," I shrugged.

"Well, I got good news for you. We have a little business to transact here, and then we'll be heading out—with you along for the ride if you get my drift." They all laughed, and one guy held his crotch.

"Of course, Sir." I was happy that these guys only thought with their dicks. "I do what I'm told."

Enrique looked up suddenly and said, "Shit. The rest of them got away while we was talking to this one."

I looked back over my shoulder and saw my Guard running into the jungle. He stopped for a second and looked back at me. With a thumb's up, he disappeared.

"Well, we gotta follow them anyway," said Enrique. "On your feet, Puta. You're gonna pay for that in more ways than I can count. When we get you back to our base, the first thing I'm going to do after we all get done balling you—and I mean all 40 of us—is to tie you down on the beach. It's crab mating time, and they'd like to pick on your flesh, I'm sure."

"Reminds me of a James Bond movie," I said.

"Yeah, '*Dr. No.*' We was watching it the other night, and it made me think that would be great torture. We'll try it out on you," said the guy called Enrique.

"Just remember what happened to Dr. No, Enrique." I snarked.

He backhanded me, and I fell back to the ground. A thin stream of blood came out of my mouth. I smiled at him. The more time we spent talking, the more time Lynn had to return to the Camp and call out reinforcements. I had thought that would be the case, anyway.

We swam across to the mainland and then went into the jungle after the others. They made me lead so that any ambush would take me out first. Enrique stayed right behind me, prodding me with his gun. After a few hundred yards, I saw what I was looking for, the dead reptilian eye watching me from its hummock. When I got near it, I tripped and fell, rolling away from the hummock. Enrique stepped between me and the hummock and raised his hand to hit me with his gun butt.

It happened so fast that none of his men saw the alligator come up and grab Enrique and drag him back underwater. "Hey, where's Enrique? Where'd the girl go?" They milled around with guns pointing in all directions.

I watched them from the spot recently vacated by the alligator. I hoped he didn't come back right away. My blonde hair floating around my head looked just like the hummock weeds, so I figured that if I didn't move, I'd be fine.

Eventually, the men moved on toward the Camp, chattering among themselves about Enrique's disappearance. Right after I left the water, I saw a swirl in it, and the alligator reappeared, with his appetite probably sated. I said a not-so-fond farewell to Enrique.

I could have used this opportunity to make a run for it. Maybe life on their ship would have been better than prison, but I had too much affection for my Guard and the other prisoners just to leave them behind. So, I quickly followed.

I caught up to the men. Their leader's loss had unnerved the remaining eleven men, and they thrashed around, cutting a wide swath across the swamp. Stepping carefully, I made a wide circle around them, almost stepping into a quicksand pool. That gave me an idea. The noise I made attracted two men, one of them the man who'd killed the Assistant Warden.

"Good. Payback time," I said to myself as I stood up and immediately fell and rolled away. Gunfire cut the jungle up where I'd been. I moaned like they'd hit me.

"Got her. We got the bitch. Let's go see if she's still alive," said one man.

Both the men walked right into the quicksand. Before they knew what was happening, they were up to their waists in it. They screamed, and two more men ran over and into the quicksand.

Five down, seven to go.

I led them a circuitous route back to the Camp, hoping that they'd cleared out. They hadn't, and I saw the reason why. The Warden and several new guards held all the Lifers and our guards at gunpoint. My Guard was lying on the ground but looked like he was breathing.

"Bastard," I said under my breath and disappeared further back into the jungle. I started to move around behind him.

Enrique's men showed up. "What the hell happened to you?" demanded the Warden.

"Enrique was bitch walking that Convict and they both disappeared. Four more of the men went off after her, and none of them's come back... You got the stuff?"

"Yes, in the airboats," and he gestured behind him. I headed in that direction and saw three airboats fully loaded with what I didn't know—or care. The Warden had left no one with the boats, so I pushed each of them off. They drifted away from the shore. I saw movement in the water, smiled, and disappeared back into the trees to return to a position right behind the Warden.

A few minutes later, the Warden leading all the prisoners and guards at gunpoint walked down from the Camp. When he saw the boats gone, he said, "Dammit. One of you go out there and get them back here."

One of his guards stepped into the water, and a giant alligator rose and pulled him in. The man screamed until he disappeared under the water; then, all you saw were a few bubbles. "It's feeding!" yelled the Warden hysterically. "One of you go in there and get a boat while it's feeding."

The Warden's guard accomplices looked around at each other and shook their heads no. The Warden shrieked at them and shot a Lifer. "Any of you that wants to get out with my men here? If yes, then swim out and bring the boats back. Or just bring one back; I don't care."

One Lifer stepped forward and into the water. She got about thigh-deep in it, and another alligator reared up and pulled her in. The screams cut off again as soon as she disappeared under the water. I felt terrible for her, but she deserved what she got.

"Dammit. 32, are you out there? If you are and don't show yourself, I'm going to kill your Guard. Yeah, I know all about the two of you. He's been porking you nicely. I've seen pictures. You should learn not to trust anyone. Out now, or he dies."

He pulled my Guard up by his shirt collar and put the gun to his head. "Now."

I stood up behind him where I had crept. "Right here, Warden, and I don't care who has pictures, you son-of-a-bitch." I knew that I'd only have seconds now, and as he turned, I punched him as the Assistant Warden had taught me, but directly in the kidneys. It was like I'd cut him down with an ax. I smiled.

My Guard rolled over and picked up the Warden's pistol. He quickly shot one man who was pointing a gun in our direction; he went down screaming. One of the good guards grabbed that man's gun, and another clubbed down one of Enrique's men. The Lifers got into it as well, swarming one accomplice and beating him senseless.

The tide had turned quickly, and I stood up and moved over to the Warden, who looked like he was about to pass out. I said, "You just don't get the chance to pass out on your own." And I kicked him in the head.

One of Enrique's men came toward me waving his rifle but stopped in horror as he looked past me. Coming up out of the water was the biggest alligator that I'd seen yet. It walked right up to me and then past me to the unconscious body of the Warden. It dragged him into the water, and just about the time his head was going under, he woke up. He was gone before he could scream.

"Looks like you have friends in reptilian places, 32," said my Guard. "I'm glad for many reasons that you came back for us."

I reached out, wrapped one arm behind his head, and pulled him close. "I wouldn't miss the next twenty-five years with you for anything." I kissed him. There was applause from guards and convicts alike.

The men were true-life pirates. Enrique and his crew had graduated from taking ships and enslaving people, though they still did some of that, to working with drug-smuggling cartels. They had made a deal with the Warden to use isolated parts of the Shepherd Island property for storage and transfer operations. They'd planned to kill all at the Camp, move the drugs, and pin it on one of the dead. This one was huge, so the landing on the barrier island.

The best-laid plans of mice and men and all. That wasn't to happen, and a large drug distribution operation was brought down with many products and a ship confiscated. The Island State Police were happy with the outcome and helped get the entire crew and the prisoners back to the Shepherd Island complex.

After returning to the prison, they took depositions from all of us Convicts, and I told them all that I had done after the pirates captured me. I'm not sure what they did with all of that, but the interrogator said to me that there would be changes here due to what happened. He also told me that they would not try me for any of the deaths I was directly involved in.

They also promoted my Guard to Assistant Warden and moved him to the Camp full time. I was unhappy. At the very least, I didn't want to have to break in a new guard, though I knew that would happen eventually, anyway. It looked like that was going to be sooner than I'd expected.

At the least, I hoped I could get myself posted to the islands project to be nearer to him. I applied for that to the new Warden.

| 7 |

Options and Choices

The Next Two Years:

They called me to the new Warden's office to meet my new Guard ostensibly. Arriving, I was asked to go into the Warden's conference room to wait. A guard took me there and asked if I wanted some water, which surprised me; I said yes. He gave me a bottle, and I was left alone, unchained, again. Something new and another surprise.

I sat and waited until the door to the Warden's office opened and an older, large man, in all ways, walked in. He was carrying a pad and a folder I saw that had my name on it. I stood up at attention, and he gestured me back to my seat. "Good afternoon, 32; I'm Warden Jeffer. I'm extremely pleased to meet you." He stuck out his hand. "You may take it, 32. Some changes are coming here, and this will be one of the first. 'When we treat people merely as they are, they will remain as they are. When we treat them as if they were

what they should be, they will become what they should be.'
That's a quote from a great religious leader from your country,
Thomas Monson."

"I know of the man, Sir. A former LDS Church President.
A complicated group of people. Not my favorites, but they've
done a lot in my former country." As soon as I spoke, I realized
that I might have offended him, and that was the last thing I
wanted to do to a man who had so much control over my life.
"I'm so sorry, Sir if I was offensive. I tend to speak my mind."

He smiled at me and waved me off. "Please, 32. I appreciate
honesty more than anything, and I don't feel that we have to
agree about everything to get along. In fact, I hope we don't
agree on everything. I want you to feel comfortable speaking
your mind. By the way, I am not an LDS Church member. I've
many of the same beliefs about them it looks like you do. That
said, when something that's said makes sense, I tend to use it."

"One of your excellent men would tell you that me speaking my mind is not a problem, I'm sure," I said.

"Ah, yes. Your Guard. Are you sad that he's left you?"

"Honestly, Sir?" I asked.

"Yes. I expect that."

"Very sad, Sir. He did a lot for me. I likely wouldn't be alive
today except for him."

"That's funny," he said. "He says the same thing about you."

He sighed. "You present an enormous problem for us, 32.
On the one hand, what you did with those pirates should mean
an immediate pardon. On the other, pardoning you would
cause a tremendous uproar, and we'd have to reveal the very

embarrassing reasons why we'd pardon you. Our Governor has left it up to me to get out of this quagmire, but I'm not sure how to do it."

"May I speak, Sir?" I asked.

"Let's get something clear, 32. Respect goes both ways. I have a lot of respect for you, and I want you to have that for me. I know that won't be easy based on what I read in your deposition about the former Warden. I want you to respect me and trust that I want you to be honest with me, polite, and respectful of my position and our relative standings, as long as that lasts." I started at that last comment. "You should always feel free to speak. I may disagree with you and decide against you, but be assured that I will hear you and explain my rationale for decisions. No more days of you defer to me and degrade yourself for my pleasure. Please understand that."

"It'll take some getting used to, Sir, but I'll try. A lot of this is inside of me, and I'll need to fix that," I stated.

"Fair enough. I want to help with that," the Warden said.

"Thank you, Sir."

"Good. What were you going to say?" he asked.

"Initially, when I was arrested and sent to the jail and then here, I thought my life was over. Now, I realize that a new door opened with that. I fully accept what I did and know that I need to spend at least twenty-two more years here before leaving. I'm okay with that but want to spend them with my Guard."

"Well, he can never be 'your' Guard again. He's now an Assistant Warden and is assigned out to the barrier island project. He'll be there for at least four more years, probably longer if the project proves successful."

"I still want to be there with him."

"Well, that may be possible. We're eliminating the Lifer Plus program and that immoral gravesite and the numbering program, effective today. You all get your names back, effective today ad new uniforms with them on them. The new Assistant Warden plans to make overtures to certain inmates and ask them if they want to work on a revised program there. It will be hard work, but the women who go there will see time taken off their sentences for their work and will have jobs after being released in the new park service we'll establish for the islands. So, if you want hard work in the sun, you can do that, Ms. McGinnis," and he smiled slightly.

"I'd almost forgotten my name. Thank you, Warden. Please call me Claire."

"Then you can call me Allen while we're together like this," he said.

"I have more to say to you, though, and want to give you an offer to consider." I nodded, and he continued, "You deserve much for what you did in the battle against the pirates. Your use of nature as a weapon was extremely creative. As I think you said to your dearly departed friend, Assistant Warden Wilson, I want to have you at my back. But, again, pardoning you is likely a bridge too far—right now, anyway. Because it would be so political, and there is still so much emotion around what you did. I'm afraid releasing you would hurt you."

"I don't want to be released, Warden. I have an obligation, and I want to pay it back," I said.

"On that. The five years added to your sentence by the former Warden was a capricious show of power to prostitute you. I eliminated those five years before I came in here today." He tapped the folder twice and then pushed it across to me. "Don't open that yet. I want to talk through this offer before you do."

"Shepherd Island has always been a prison. First for escaped slaves and then for people adjudicated by the courts. As I think you know, it has a warranted reputation as a harsh place and the Camp the most brutal places. Year after year, our internal audit services rate the place slightly better than a sewer. Sometimes, worse than that. The State has failed its citizens and its obligation to you significantly by allowing this to happen. One thing your case did was to throw a very unforgiving light on conditions here. The State is committed now, and in my opinion belatedly, to fix that. We will place a significant focus on rehabilitation and studying and addressing recidivism, which is substantial in your community. I will captain that and am looking for someone to help me assess and manage the issues here. That would be the position I want to offer you. You've shown, more than amply, that you can be trusted and no longer need that." And he pointed to the collar, took out a small black unit, pressed a button, and the collar opened. He held out his hand, and I took it off and handed it to him. He clicked it shut and put it aside.

"Whatever you decide, whether it is to stay here and to work with me or to work on the island project, your status is changing. This is entirely within my control span, so today, you're becoming a Trusty, only our second Trusty so far. I believe you met our barber; he's the other one. That will mean that you'll have the freedom to move as you want to within the grounds and be seen as a leader among the administration and prisoners alike. You may also leave the prison under supervision. That is for your protection more than anything else. But you'll not be restrained in any way. I hope that you appearing in public more and more will make society more comfortable with you, and eventually, we'll be able to release you. Hopefully, well before your twenty years have expired. Please look at the document," he said.

It was a massive change for me, and I sat back, trying to absorb it. It laid out my two options and my future. It set out that they considered me a junior member of the staff with any citizen's rights and obligations until I violated a rule as laid out in the document. The Court of Appeals could only withdraw privileges after careful adjudication. He'd taken me out from under the thumb of fickle prison administrators. I was also to be paid for my work, including room and board with an apartment furnished by the prison on the grounds. My salary would be banked to be used in the prison store or withdrawn for trips into the community. While on prison grounds, I would wear the new prison Trusty uniform, and when I left the prison, I could wear street clothes and, again, move unrestrained, but with some supervision initially.

"Can I take this, Sir, and talk to someone?" I asked.

"Of course." He looked at his watch and said, "He's likely waiting for you outside."

I tried out my new privileges right away. My Guard and I went to Reception and asked for access to my suitcases. Of course, almost nothing fit me, as I had grown since being in prison, putting on a lot of muscle and bulk. So, I put on a tee-shirt, a pair of gym shorts and a pair of sandals. We walked out, for the first time in years, with me a somewhat freer woman.

The first thing we did was to head over to my Guard's apartment. It had been closed since this rotation, so it was musty. He apologized. "Oh, please shut up and make love to me like I want to make to you."

After we did and were lying in bed, I brought out the folder and recapped my conversation with the Warden. "Seems like a good man, though trust is hard-won with me," I said.

"He's a good man, Claire, with a great reputation. Was the Governor here several terms back and tried to address the problems with the prison system. I think he has the leverage to do that now," said Lynn.

"How'd he get that? It would have been easy for the State to sweep all of this under the carpet. Why now?" I asked.

"Who knows, maybe someone has an ear in high places," Lynn said.

There was a knock at his door, and he put on a robe and went to get it. A few minutes later, he walked in with the Warden. "I'd like to introduce you to my uncle, Claire."

I was sitting up in the bed with the sheets pulled up around my neck, looking back and forth between the two men. The Warden smiled at me. "I heard about your problem with clothes, so I did a little shopping in my daughter's closet and brought you some things. Here." He pulled in a small roller suitcase and set it in the room. "I'll wait for the two of you in the living room. Lynn, this place smells like a tomb."

We talked for several hours and came up with a solution. I would work on both jobs. I liked to work a lot, and I didn't want to lose the outdoor work that I'd been doing at the Camp and thought that the study work that the Warden wanted to do could benefit from my experience and talents. They were both reluctant, but when I said I'd be home every night to my Guard, he gave in. The Warden did soon afterward.

Every day, early, Trusty Claire traveled with the Assistant Warden to join her workmates on the island project. They realized they had a celebrity with them and were supportive in all the ways they needed to be. The typical workday was 13 hours on the islands, but I had to leave early to make it back to the prison. I left the team after about 10 hours and then returned to the prison where I changed clothes and then started my second job, usually leaving that around midnight when the airboat would take me back to the inlet just below the Camp headquarters.

Weekends were a bit different. Island project work was for only 8 hours each day, and the Warden didn't need me for the other job. So, my Guard and I had time to go into town and spend it there. I kept myself out of sight mainly because when I was out shopping with my Guard, a family member of the man who had died attacked me. He was arrested, but I refused to press charges. It reinforced to all of them they needed to work me in to the community very gradually.

Over about six months, the Warden gave me complete control over the recidivism project. I reported to him and the other leaders regularly, but he let me do what I thought was right to collect data and then develop program proposals to reduce recidivism. Several of these were very successful, though we wouldn't know their full effects for a few years yet. One work-study program placed inmates into internships with local businesses. The business paid the inmate a half salary and got a devoted worker. The inmates got, maybe two to three times what they made at the prison, thus had plenty of money for themselves.

At the end of a two-year test period, it had proven very successful. Several of these inmates had not spent a continuous period out of prison more than eight months in many years.

| 8 |

Forced Family

The Next Three Years:

After the incident in town, I decided I needed to meet face-to-face with the family of the man who had died of COVID-19. No one thought this was a good idea, but I was adamant, feeling that I'd never be able to be safe on the outside if I didn't get them to put their anger behind them. I realized that would be painful for me, highly likely, but I was committed.

A meeting was set up with the Domínguez family in one of the courthouse conference rooms after court hours. The family members, six of them, were led into the conference room. I was already there with my hands cuffed and locked to the center of the table. I had dressed in one of my older Lifer outfits that displayed the brands on my chest.

"Good evening. I think you know who I am. Could I know your names, please?" I asked.

"The only person you need to know, Convict, is this young man," said an older man. "This is my son's boy. You took his father's life. His name is Alejandro, and he has some things he wants to get satisfaction about."

The boy, maybe 12 years old if I recollected right but big for his age, came up out of the family group. He looked back at them, and they all filed out of the room, leaving the two of us alone. "So, according to my grandfather, you are the arrogant Puta who took my father from me. Is that true?"

"I can't say whether it was me, but I've taken responsibility for it and have been jailed for it for life, as you can see by this brand," I said.

The boy reached out to touch me, and I reared back. "Alejandro, there's supposed to be no physical contact between us. That was part of the deal for us to talk. Please stand on the other side of the table."

"Yes, and I understand that there are only the two of us here. Right, Convict?" He reached out to stroke my hair. "Such pretty blonde hair. You didn't answer my question. We're alone, correct?"

"Yes, we are, Alejandro," I answered, now thinking I might have made a mistake in setting up this meeting.

"Good." He sat down on the table right next to me with his leg touching my leg. "I never knew my mother. She left us right after I was born. My father was all I had, and I thought we were best for each other. I know you're working hard to make things right for what you did, and I am glad you do that."

He caressed my hair again, "But I'm still missing a parent...I want you to be my mother."

I was shocked and sat back in my chair. "Alejandro, I don't know what to say. I'm a prisoner. I can't take you in. You can't live in prison with me."

"My grandfather told me you'd say something like that, but he asked our lawyer to look at what it means to be a Trusty, even if a Lifer. You have a lot of freedom, they say, and can do this. My grandfather told me to tell you that if you do not, you will never get out of prison to be with that man you call Your Guard, even if his uncle is the big man he is. My grandfather is a big man as well."

He got up off the table and walked out. A few minutes later, Judge Sutton entered the room with Anthony Hodgins and another man they introduced as Mr. Herrera, the Domínguez family attorney. "Good evening, Claire. It's good to see you again looking so well after, what, five years?"

"Just about, yes, Judge; good to see you too," I said. My head was still spinning from my conversation with the boy.

"I want to compliment you on the progress you've made with your rehabilitation. Your behavior and commitment to making good for your crimes haven't gone unnoticed, as I know you're aware. You've just talked with Alejandro Domínguez, and I believe he's made his family's proposal to you. Mr. Herrera has done the research and found the law that would allow you to adopt Alejandro and for him to be with you in prison. It would be a fully legal adoption, with four pro-visos stipulated in the papers that Mr. Herrera has drawn up, that are legal but may or may not be acceptable to you." She looked a little sad about all of this.

Anthony picked up from her. "The proposal is that, as you have already heard, you adopt Alejandro as your child. Second, he would be your only child, ever. The family wants to have your attention undivided on raising Alejandro, as they believe it is only right. Third, the family would comprise only you and Alejandro, so again your attention can be undivided. Fourth, you are responsible, on your own, for the funding of Alejandro's schooling and lifestyle until he reaches his majority or you pass, whichever comes first."

"As you're, I'm sure, thinking there is more to this than simply undivided attention, and Mr. Domínguez wants to punish and keep you on the brink of poverty and unable to complete your commitment to paying off the $10,000 fine for years to come," said Anthony.

"It is an entirely fair proposal, Ms. McGinnis," said Herrera. "You took away any chance of happiness from Alejandro. My client feels that the same thing should happen to you."

"Don't my years in prison and current status mean anything? The State feels that I have given back and deserve recognition for that. Doesn't that count?" I asked, now nearing tears.

"We're not asking for any change of your status, but for you to commit to raising Mr. Domínguez's grandson in the manner his father would have and with the same commitment to the boy," said Herrera.

"May I speak to my attorney?" I asked.

"Yes, of course, but this deal disappears tonight if you do not agree to it," said Herrera. He rose to leave.

"May I stay, too, Claire?" said Judge Sutton.

"Yes, please," I said.

After Herrera had left, I asked, "Can they do this to me? I've fallen in love and hoped that I might finally have a settled life. Yes, as a Trusty, but a married one with a man who I've come to love," I said.

"Here's the problem, Claire," began Hodgins. "They can propose any contract they want. It's up to you to accept or reject it, but you can be sure that they'll make these last few years look easy if you don't accept their proposal. The Domínguez family is enormously powerful, and the grandfather is one of the biggest business competitors to the Artigas family. They cannot get to Hector, so they're coming after you."

"You have already done five years of the 20-year sentence, Claire," said Judge Sutton. "You would need to put your life back on hold again for nine years until the boy is 21. I realize that is a long time, and you will have a tough conversation with your friend about that, but this is a deal that will ensure that you remain on the path that you've put yourself on."

"I can't ask Lynn to wait for me for nine years. That would be unfair. Not seeing him for all those years just will not work." After a pause as I considered options, I asked, "But I don't have much choice, do I?"

"Not if you want to have the freedom and excellent prospects you have," said the Judge.

I wanted to blame the Domínguez's, but I realized I had only myself to blame for all of this. I cried and cried. The Judge and Anthony left me to my thoughts and the phone call to make to Lynn. About thirty minutes later, I opened the door to Herrera, Sutton, Hodgins, and a smirking Alejandro. "I'm ready to sign the papers," I said.

"Oh, Mom. I am so happy," said Alejandro. His smile was ingenuine, and his eyes were cold.

Herrera provided a written summary of the agreement that he had me sign in addition to the contract documents; it had seven significant warrants:

- You are adopting Alejandro Domínguez, who, from this day forward, will be Alejandro McGinnis, your only and legally adopted child.
- He will live with you as would your naturally born son until his majority. You will ensure that he is clothed and equipped according to his desires and needs. He is the sole judge relative to what his wants and needs are.
- As your son, Alejandro will be the sole beneficiary of all assets you currently or will ever hold upon your death or as otherwise provided here.
- Until Alejandro reaches his majority, you will singularly focus on his upbringing. There will be no distractions aside from those posed by your work as a Trusty.
- You will ensure that Alejandro will continue with his private schooling and participate in all his extracurricu-

lar activities. You will join as his parent in these at his request.

- Alejandro will be able to continue to interact with his family. You shall not move away from the Island without agreement from the family.
- You will provide an allowance to Alejandro equal to 50% of your current salary.

We will automatically deem any failure to comply with these warrants an offense under State Law, punishable with a 5-year mandatory sentence, which you agree will be in addition to any currently unexpired term of imprisonment.

I again felt that all the progress I'd made was being flushed away, but I signed anyway and said, "Alejandro, let's go home." We left and took a van back to the prison.

When we arrived back at my studio apartment on the prison grounds, Alejandro walked over to the bed, threw his bag on it, and said, "Where do you sleep, Mom? Do we sleep together?"

"No, I'll sleep on the sofa," I said.

"I have to go to work in the morning, and you have to go to school. Go to sleep. Good night." He opened his bag, took off his clothes, and fell into bed, completely naked.

I went to my wardrobe drawer and took out a nightgown, and went into the bathroom to change. When I came out, I told Alejandro that I left early every morning to go to work and would not be back usually until close to midnight. He screwed his face up and acted sad. "No, Mom. I want you to be here for me when I go to school in the morning and come back at night. You need to help me with homework and, as this agreement says, be available for school events, sports, and other things. I'll give you a couple of days to work this out, but if I'm not happy, I'll call my grandfather."

"The little bastard would do that too," I thought.

"They've got me over a barrel, Lynn," I said. Allen was with me in his office talking to Lynn over a video link out to the Camp. "If I don't do this, I'll be imprisoned forever; they will see to it. Judge Sutton as much as said that."

"I know old man Domínguez," said Allen. "He's a tough customer who we've been trying to get in here for years. Maybe it's time to ramp up that effort. I'll see what I can do. In the meantime, though, Claire is right; there's little we can do. Claire, you'll have to stop your trips to the Camp for the time being. The good news in this is for me: I'll get your brilliant talents on the recidivism project full-time. I'll also require you to take one hour off four times a day to exercise in the staff gym, so you keep that little body Lynn so loves to get into nice and tight."

I blushed bright red, "Thanks, Warden. I think."

When I arrived home that night, I found the apartment trashed and Alejandro drinking one of my beers. When I yelled at him, he said, "Yell at me and see what happens. Do you think this is a regular parent-child thing? You're sadly mistaken. Come over here and help with my homework." He patted the bed next to him.

"No way. Get over to this table right now. Don't fuck with me, young man, or I'll tan your hide. Remember where I've been for the past five years. Any time I stepped out of line, I got these." I pulled my tank top up, and he saw the scars and brands. His eyes bugged out, and he quickly gathered his books and came over to the kitchen table. We worked shoulder to shoulder on his homework. He wasn't completely dumb, but I saw he would need a lot of focus.

After the homework, we walked to the front of the prison and took a bus into town. We had something to eat and shopped for food. When we were heading to bed, he again asked, "Could you sleep with me? I just need a warm body by my side. Please."

"I will because the couch is damned uncomfortable, but you remember who I am and keep your hands to yourself. I promise I'll take my belt to you if you don't."

"Yes, Mom." Apparently, my tough stand meant something to him. The sarcasm was gone, replaced by respect, and we slept well that night and many after that. I woke the following day to his arm wrapped around me, and he nestled into my back, sleeping peacefully.

Thus began an interesting and the best of friendships.

Alejandro required a lot of attention. His father had not paid him much and allowed him to run wild. Of course, living inside prison walls meant he had many rules to live by. He seemed to flourish under the structure, and his grades improved at school. The fees for that were being deducted directly from my pay, and I would have been broke if Allen had not given me a raise that kept me whole after deducting Alejandro's expenses. Domínguez meant what he said about keeping me on the brink of poverty. That said, Alejandro turned out to be reasonable and wanted to help where he could, and he did.

About four months after acquiring my new family, Allen invited us over to dinner. He said that he wanted to see the boy and take his measure. It was a surprisingly successful night. Alejandro had never eaten out in polite settings. He knew that and leaned over to me early on and said, "Can you help? I don't know what to do with all these different utensils." I smiled at him and said yes. He had so much to learn to fit into polite society.

At the end of the evening, the Warden said to him, "I know your grandfather, Alejandro, and I am happy to say you're nothing like him." Alejandro said that he didn't know how to take that. "You're a good boy. I will talk to your mother tomorrow about an idea I have for some things for you to do around the prison so you can contribute."

Like the first time I heard myself called 32, hearing Allen call me "mother" made me feel quite different, but positively this time. I smiled at him. His driver took us back to the prison.

"You need to get ready for school, young man," I said to him the following day and ruffled his hair. "Go take a shower and get dressed. We can take the bus into town together if you want me to come with you." I'd started taking the prison bus to town and then walking him to school, but I could see that might start embarrassing him. On the way back, I'd shop for food. At night, I'd, mostly, pick him up, and when I couldn't, the Warden had told his driver that he should help. The driver had been with the Warden for over 20 years and was a delightful older man. Alejandro thought it was cool being picked up in a limo. A win-win. This went on for several months more. Alejandro and I settled into a rhythm that fulfilled me, and I thought it did him as well.

I missed Lynn much, but the relationship with Alejandro that we had established had become more and more fulfilling to me. I was up early the morning after our dinner with Allen doing some work and having a video call with Lynn at the Camp, as had become our custom. Alejandro had taken to getting up early as well, and he came out to the small terrace behind our apartment and sat next to me.

"Who's this?" he asked.

"Lynn Jeffer. He's the Assistant Warden out at our island reclamation project. Say good morning to my son, Alejandro, Lynn."

"Good morning, son. Glad to meet you." He said that without a trace of sarcasm.

"What's an island reclamation project, Mom?"

I went into a lengthy explanation of the project and its importance for the Island and our survival. I could see that as we talked, he became more and more intrigued and engaged. Lynn and I looked at each other, telegraphing that we may have taken an essential first step in getting back together. He had many questions, and I left him talking to Lynn when I went in to take a shower and prepared to start the day.

At 10 AM, I had my regular morning staff meeting with the Warden and the leadership staff. My piece of the meeting was to talk about the rehabilitation and recidivism project. Initially, some of the older prison leadership put the project down and treated me like a third-class citizen. Some of those men were gone, and others had taken to me because of the pirates. Even though they talked about a lot, some of which I felt nervous about—specifically prisoner disciplinary issues—the Warden ordered me to stay for all of it. "Part of the job of a Trusty, Claire. You have to get used to this.," he said. Sometimes the attendees even solicited my opinion on these matters. Even though I wore a Trusty uniform that hid my brands, they knew what I was. I gradually became an accepted member of the team.

Toward the end of the meeting, the Warden asked me to stay behind. "I heard from Lynn that you, he, and the boy had a friendly conversation this morning. He said that Alejandro seemed to be taken by the island project. Do you think he was?"

"Definitely, Warden," I said.

"Good. I wanted to brainstorm some ideas this morning about getting him engaged positively here, anyway. I'm going to order you to spend weekends at the Camp from now on, from Friday night through Sunday night, with the boy. That hard work will be good for him as long as we make him feel that there's something that he can own."

"I'll talk with Lynn about that, Sir."

"Good. Now get back to work, Convict," he said with a smile. I smiled back and returned to my research tasks.

That was Monday morning, and I let Alejandro know about my orders and that he would need to come with me on Friday. He was excited. "Wow, a road trip with Mom. So cool," he said. Over the next four days, his excitement grew.

Thursday and Friday were school holidays, so Alejandro hung around the apartment. I asked if he wanted to work out with me. "I've never done anything like that," he said. "What do you have here?"

"Well, there's a track around the inside of the fence, weights, bags, a boxing ring…." I said.

"Really, a ring?" he asked.

"Yup, some prisoners like to box. A few of the guards manage it. We'd be inside the prison proper, so you'd have to be extra careful, and I would need to get permission for you, but I bet they'd like you. I work out at 9 AM, 12 PM, 2 PM, and 4 PM, for an hour each time," I said.

"Wow, that's a lot. Do you fight?" he asked.

"Sometimes. There are a couple of the girls who I've known for years, and we like to mix it up," I said.

"Will I be able to watch it?"

"Well, you gotta be there to do that. What do you say? I work out hard, and I'll make you sweat," I said.

"Sure, I guess," the boy said.

At 9 AM, he was waiting outside the administration building. I'd gotten permission from the Warden to bring him inside, and he was excited. Alejandro didn't expect the workout to be so hard. He was soaked and exhausted when we finished. "Come back at noon, and my friend Paola said she'd fight me, and you could watch. She says she wants to beat my ass in front of you. We'll see. She's good, but I'm better."

At noon, Alejandro was waiting outside my office, practically hopping from foot to foot. "He *is* a kid," I thought and smiled. I had changed into my gym clothes in my office and brought out my boxing gloves. "We both use 16 oz gloves, so we don't damage each other too much. Also, use these," and I showed him my headgear, "And this." I showed him the mouth guard. "Let's go workout."

We worked out for half an hour with Paola, who I wanted to get into the Trusty program. Paola herself didn't care either way. The prison was her life, and she'd accepted that. "So, this your boy? What's your name, boy?" she asked.

"Alejandro, ma'am," he answered.

"Been a long time since someone called me something other than Convict or worse. I ain't no ma'am. Never had a chance to have a kid. I envy your Mom, but I'm still going to beat the shit out of her. Call me Paola," Paola said.

We climbed into the ring. We did full-contact mixed martial arts type of boxing, so while the gloves afforded some protection, feet and knees were bare and weapons in and of themselves. We went at each other for a half-hour, and in the last moments, Alejandro yelled, "Great fight, Mom."

That distracted me and allowed Paola to land a combination that sent me to the mat. I popped back up, shook my head twice, and launched into a series of punches and kicks that drove Paola back into the ropes. Both of us were still standing when the final bell rang, but it was clear that I was holding my friend up. They pointed the fight to a draw, and we hugged each other. "Next time, bitch," said Paola, "you'll stay down."

"In your dreams, Paola. See you next week," I said.

"That was awesome, Mom. Thanks for taking me. My grandfather runs a few what they call cage fight rings around town. They're a lot more brutal than this, but not nearly as beautiful. You and Paola are graceful, like dancers," said Alejandro.

"Thanks, Son. I need to get a shower back in the building, and you need to get back to the house to do the same. Race you to the exit."

The airboat docks were at the rear of the prison property but outside of the fence. I had to show my I.D. and the permission slip signed by the Warden for Alejandro to travel with me. I was wearing my Lifer uniform that showed my brands, which I wore when I met Alejandro. By policy, I needed to be cuffed during the trip to the islands, but the guard who piloted the boat just told us to sit as he usually did with me when we traveled there alone.

"Marco, you need to cuff me," I said.

He looked at me and the boy who was gaping and said, "I didn't want to do that to you while your boy was here, Claire. We all know you're the furthest thing from a flight risk."

"Thanks, Marco, but the rules are the rules, and Alejandro must understand his mother fully."

Marco shrugged, came forward, cuffed my hands behind me, and then linked the cuffs to a bolt in the boat's floor. He smiled sadly at me. "You know, you're a masochist, don't you? You're better than most of the guards around here."

"Thanks, Marco, but that's because I've accepted what I am," I said.

He looked at me sternly and, with no trace of a smile, said, "And we know who you are. Some of us wouldn't be here if it weren't for your bravery. You have our respect and love."

We took off for the hour ride to the islands. Alejandro was as attentive as Marco, and I described what he was seeing and what he would see. As night approached, Marco stopped the boat, and as we usually did, we ate dinner under the stars.

"Mr. Marco, how does my mother eat if she's chained like that."

"I normally give her bits of food. Do you want to do that?"

"Yes. Is that okay, Mom?"

I smiled and shook my head yes. He fed me with a sad look on his face.

We arrived at the islands around 11 PM. Marco unchained me, and another guard led me off to be with the prisoners. Alejandro started to leave the boat, but Marco stopped him. "No, son, your mother stays here with the prisoners. We're going to the Camp. You'll be back in the morning. Have a seat."

With tears in his eyes, Alejandro turned and said, "I don't want to leave my Mom."

I turned and smiled at Alejandro. "Go with him, Alejandro. That's the deal for you being able to be out here. The Assistant Warden is waiting for you and will bring you back tomorrow so you can see our work and help out."

After the pirate invasion and Lynn assuming the job of Assistant Warden in charge of the Camp and project, he made several changes there. First, he changed the name to the Barrier Islands Reclamation Project from the Justus Angel and Mistress L. Horry Camp. The name changes alone signaled a monumental shift in attitudes toward the convicts working there. He also made some changes to the prisoners' accommodations when they were working. Tents replaced the poles to which prisoners were chained. They did not lock prisoners up at night because, in part, running away would be suicide and because they were now all volunteers and were being rewarded substantially for the work. So, me being led away in chains was a bit of a show for Alejandro.

After the airboat departed, the guard unlocked my cuffs and chains before we reached the tents. "Are we going to have to do this every time he comes out here?" he asked.

"Hopefully, not after this time."

"Great. I had to dig these things up from storage."

The prisoners and guards were sitting around a fire, talking and sipping various beverages. When I came into the light, several of them jumped up to give me hugs and kisses. "Wonderful to see you, Claire. We'd heard that you might not be coming back out here and were all upset by that. Besides, you being gone makes the work a lot harder for all of us. Are you staying?"

"Sorry, I can't," and I told them about Alejandro.

As a result, they were ready to meet Alejandro the following day when he arrived with Lynn. When they walked up out of the water—Lynn took him through the jungle on the same route I'd taken when I led the pirates around—Alejandro started to run up to me. Lynn grabbed him. "Sorry, buddy, but you can't talk to your mother at least right now."

"Why not?" he asked.

"Because they're getting their duties for the day. You need to understand that your Mom is probably stronger than any three of these women and maybe the men too. There are many reasons for that, some of them not so nice, but she craves this work. The harder, the better for her. Once she gets her assignment, I'll let you talk to her. That's why the Warden has her working out four times a day back at the prison. If he didn't, and we didn't, she'd probably go crazy."

The guard who was giving out the responsibilities finished his assignments, and I went to pick up a shovel, pick, and several other tools. I had a focused look on my face and smiled at the thought of two days' excruciating work. Alejandro ran up to me and gave me a big hug. "Hi, Mom. I had a great night with the Assistant Warden." He leaned in and whispered, "Is he the one you love?"

I grinned and said, "Yes, Alejandro. And the one I cannot have."

"Well, I like him, and I'm going to talk to my grandfather."

"Don't do that, son. I'm not sure how he'd react if he knew you'd met him," I said.

"I hear you, Mom. I like Lynn, and it is not fair that you're not together. I'm going to, anyway. I don't care what grandfather thinks."

I looked at Lynn and shrugged. They must have had a hell of a night together.

"Now, where are we going to work?" he asked.

"Over here," I said. "The work is hard and hot, but we're doing great things out here. Like Lynn explained to you, these islands we're building will keep the seas away from our homes on the Island. It's significant work and a great science project."

"Great. I came to be with you. I know I'm not as strong as you are, but I want to pull some of your load. Lynn and I talked about that, and he said no at first, but you know me, I can be convincing. I'm staying out here with you all tonight as well. If you fight about it, I'll get Lynn to order it." He laughed, and we went off to work.

Alejandro worked hard, shoulder to shoulder, with me. I initially gave him simple jobs, but as the day went on, I found he was a self-starter and quickly expected what was needed, where, and when. Lunch packs were distributed around 1 PM, and we had an hour to eat them and rest. I used the time to introduce Alejandro to the other women. It was interesting; he was respectful and friendly to all of them, even the women who sported the Lifer and Lifer plus brands like me. They responded in kind, and I saw some relationships sprouting.

At 2 PM, we started working again and moved earth until about an hour after sunset. My first 13-hour day in some time, and I was invigorated by it. Alejandro slept beside me, exhausted, he said, and once again, I awoke to find his arm around me, and him snuggled close. Every morning I woke to see him like that made me smile and be sad at the same time. I desperately wanted a child but knew Domínguez had taken that away from me, along with many other things. Maybe forever by the time my deal with him was up.

"Mom, can we talk?" Alejandro asked over breakfast. After I shook my head, yes, he started, "I want you to let me finish what I am going to say. Don't interrupt, please, Convict." He smiled and continued, "When we met, I think you know I wanted to hurt you. My grandfather encouraged me. He even said he wanted me to make you do, well, bad things to me so we could get you into more trouble. That night when you showed me your brands and scars and told me you'd tan my hide if I touched you in a bad way was the start of a change in me. My teachers at school said it was 'setting boundaries.' I've never had boundaries. When my dad was alive, he let me do what I wanted. I've figured out that wasn't for any parenting reason, but because he was lazy and all about himself. Kind of like those pictures and documentaries I saw about you. He was, what was the word they used...."

"Entitled," I said.

"Yes, as entitled as you said you were, and I believe you felt you were. Now that I see who you are and what you've done with yourself, I know what we did is wrong. So, I am going back to my grandfather to tell him I want out and to return home. I also will tell him I want him to leave you alone," Alejandro said.

"Oh, Alejandro. I don't know what to say, except that I won't let you leave me. You're part of me now," I said.

"I guess we talk to him together, then," he said, sounding equal parts happy and relieved that I wanted him.

"For a twelve-year-old boy...," I thought.

Even though I was a Trusty, I couldn't have a phone. I could use one of the prison phones that were all monitored, but I had not in years since I had no one to call. My father had told me they never wanted to see or hear from me again the last time we spoke years before. I had called to apologize for what I'd done and to, hopefully, get some emotional support from them. My Aunt made it all about her as she always did, saying she'd lost so much sleep worrying about me and would waste no more. My mother wouldn't even speak to me, and my father railed and railed about my selfishness. He told me he had always known I would never amount to anything, and I'd gone and proven it. I tried to make him understand. I knew that I'd been selfish, but he would only hear what he had to say. He hung up on me, and that was the last time I'd talked to any of my family. As I look back on it, now, good riddance, I say.

Alejandro's cell phone, which was a brand new high-end one that I thought looked like a piece of candy, fascinated me. "Grandfather, I want to talk to you about my mother and the deal you forced her into. We want to have a meeting with you here at the prison."

Alejandro listened politely for a few minutes and then said, "She's been more a parent to me in the last six months than anyone in the Domínguez family has ever been. You will see her and me, or you will regret it deeply."

I heard his grandfather screaming at him over the telephone. "She's a prisoner, Grandfather, and just cannot come to you when you order it. Be here tomorrow at 11 AM at the Warden's conference room." He hung up as his grandfather continued to rant at him.

"Well, that went very well, I think," he said. "Let's finish my homework, and then we can play some chess."

I had taught Alejandro to play chess and was impressed with how fast he'd picked it up. He enjoyed evaluating the options and anticipating his opponent's—usually my—moves. He rarely won when we first started playing weeks before; now, he rarely lost. He enjoyed, he said, anticipating his opponent—especially me. Now, though, his opponent was his grandfather, and I hoped he hadn't overplayed this.

The following day, I met with the Warden before our 10 AM meeting and let him know about Alejandro's conversation with his grandfather the night before.

"Well. The young man has balls, that's for sure. Marcelo Domínguez is one of the worst crime bosses on the island. Not a man to be trifled with. Your boy must have a lot on him."

"Alejandro wants our 10 AM meeting to run over this morning, so his grandfather is livid by the time he gets in here. And if you could be nearby, that might be good too," I said.

"Of course, I wouldn't miss this for the world. Remember that everything that goes on here's monitored. I hope the son of a bitch implicates himself."

At almost noon, the 10 AM meeting ended, and the leadership filed out past a very irritated Marcelo Domínguez, who stormed into the room past them, with Herrera in tow. Alejandro had been waiting in the Warden's office, having taken the day off from school. He came in through that doorway.

"Good day, grandfather. Many thanks for coming to visit my mother and me here," he said.

"And I'm sorry," I said, "we were delayed in getting with you, but the Warden had a lengthy agenda for our daily leadership meeting this morning. He says hello and gives his best wishes."

"Tell the old bastard I will someday feast on his liver," said Domínguez. His lawyer looked up, shocked, and shook his head no.

"Mr. Domínguez, we came to listen, not to create animosity. Let us listen to what Alejandro and the Convict have to say," said Herrera.

Alejandro rounded on the attorney, pulling out the original agreement summary, "I will ask politely, once, Mr. Herrera and Grandfather, that you refer to my mother as my mother or Ms. McGinnis. You coerced her into signing this contract, did you not? You forced her to adopt me, which makes her my mother. My family. Really, my only family when I look at it. So, you treat her with respect, or I'll consider that a violation of the contract, not that we have any breach consequences on our side. I'm sure, though, the courts might find your berating her and how you engineered all of this at least a moral issue."

Both the men sat there silent.

"I will take that as agreement."

"No, you will take that as sil...." started Herrera, but a wave from Domínguez stopped him.

"Well played, Grandson. My apologies, Ms. McGinnis. You have done marvelous things with your son. Now, what do you want, Alejandro?"

"Three things, grandfather: First, I want you to terminate this agreement. I want my mother to be my mother because she wants to be my mother, not because you forced me down her throat. Second, I want you to release my Trust to her control and administration. Third, I don't want to see you or any of the family ever again."

Marcelo Domínguez looked at the boy and considered for a moment, "What do I get out of this?"

"My complete respect and continuing respect as long as you live," said Alejandro. Something passed between his grandfather and him, and he sighed. "Also, if anything were to happen to my mother or me, I have made sure that my legacy will live after me, well us."

"There is a flaw in your plans, Alejandro," said Herrera. "Your mother, this woman, is a convict doing life for the death of your father. The courts would never permit her to be the administrator of your Trust."

"That may be correct, Mr. Herrera, but we have some very powerful people on our side who can probably help here. Also, if they cannot, by terminating the contract my mother signed, she will be able to marry the man she loves, and he could become the administrator."

"Who is that? Some ex-con?" asked Herrera.

"No, the Warden's nephew."

Domínguez raised his hand. "I will only do this if you promise me two things, Ms. McGinnis."

"This is between me and you, Grandfather."

"Please, Alejandro, let me speak. Despite what you may see here, I have an immense amount of affection for my grandson. I meant this relationship I forced to be a learning opportunity for him, and that it indeed has been. I'm pleased about that; you've done very well in a brief time. For that, I thank you."

"Alejandro, I will agree to the spirit what you ask for, but I want to see you from time to time, but with your mother present. Second, Ms. McGinnis—can I call you Claire?"

"Yes, of course," I said.

"You have proven to be nothing like what I had thought you'd be. Maybe you were once, but now you're a serious, sincere, and loving mother. So, I offer my apologies for what I did and said, but I think it has worked out well for all of us, has it not, Lifer?" He smiled. I did too. "I truly want to see you from time to time outside of here so we can continue as a family. That includes you, too, of course, Claire."

"Being here in this prison makes me extremely nervous as I am sure your Warden would like to see me inside its walls. Correct, Warden?... So, I will leave. Now."

He smiled. "Mr. Herrera will draw up the termination papers and get them to you later today." He stood up, and we all did. "My very best wishes to you all and you too, Warden," he said, looking around the room.

As soon as they left, the door opened, and the Warden came in. He looked at Alejandro. "Are you sure you're only 12, young man?"

"Actually, Warden, I'm 13."

"What, when was your birthday, Alejandro?" I asked.

"The first day we met."

"Well," said the Warden, "you certainly impressed me today, young man."

"It is amazing, sir, what you can do when you have an incentive." He smiled at me. "Can I take my mother out for the day, Warden?"

He looked at his watch and said, "It's a little early, but yes. What did you have in mind?"

"It's a surprise, Sir."

"Okay, then. Surprise her away." He completed a pass order for me to be released in my son's custody, which I would have found funny if it weren't so degrading.

"Where are we going, Alejandro? I need to know how to dress."

"We're going out to lunch, and then I want to take you to my school. Can you wear your Lifer uniform?"

I stopped, stunned. "What are you talking about? You want me to go out with you wearing my Lifer uniform so I can go to your school and be humiliated? What are you thinking?" I asked, very upset.

"No, no, Mom. Everyone at school knows I live here at the prison, and they know who you are. What I want you to show them is who you *really* are. Give them a chance to know you as I do. There's a part two of this that I talked with Lynn about. I want to bring the class to the islands to work there on weekends. He thought it would be a 'noble' thing to do, he said. It would be great for prisoner rehabilitation and the students and then maybe their families to see all of you as less evil. Plus, we all can take part in a real, practical science project."

"You're something, Son. I need to get my head into this, though. Why today? Just because we're on a roll?" I asked.

"Something like that, yeah. But many people are talking about me and what goes on here. I was hoping you could set the record straight with them and interest them in coming to work on the islands with us. I ask you to tell them your whole story, not the B.S. that was on those shows and websites and not the sex or dirty stuff, but about how someone like you ends up in a place like this," he said. "Can you do that for me, Mom?"

"There was a T.V. show in the U.S. once called '*Scared Straight.*' Sort of like that then?"

"Yeah, but I want people to understand also why I love you."

I put on my Lifer uniform that showed off my brands and left the prison for the town on the prison bus. Alejandro took me to a small restaurant near his school that his schoolmates frequented. Several were there and waved when we came in. He waved back, and we took a table and ordered.

"I've got this, Mom. Grandfather gave me some cash before he left," said Alejandro.

"I'm glad you did because while I have a bank account at the prison, I'm not allowed to carry cash at the prison. We left so fast; I didn't have time to withdraw any. They say if there's cash around, prisoners will steal it or worse. I've never seen that. Another urban legend about us convicts and our missing moral decency," I said.

"Hello, Alejandro. Who's the hot, sexy girl you're with?" asked someone from behind me.

"My Mother, Arturo."

I heard a gulping sound and turned to see three boys, each a shade of red darker than the other.

"I'm so sorry, Mrs. McGinnis. You don't look like an adult from behind."

"It's okay, Arturo. Maybe you better stop before you get into more trouble. Please call me Claire. I'm not a Mrs.," I said.

Alejandro introduced the other two boys, David Moreno and Nil Arriaga. The three stood and talked with us until our meals came and then returned to their table to finish their meals.

"Nice boys, but they couldn't stop looking down the front of my uniform. They made me feel like I was on sale," I said.

Alejandro started to get up, "I'll say something to them."

"No, you won't. Sit down and eat," I said. "This is my cross to bear. I appreciate your wanting to protect me, Alejandro, but I need to learn how to handle this if I spend more time outside. Besides, that's what these old uniforms were all about. Degrade the Convict; take away every shred of self-worth and decency. I'm climbing back up again, Son, and I do need your help, but let me handle this one."

They ate in companionable silence. From time to time, I would look up at the reflection in the mirror behind Alejandro to see the boys staring at me and talking among themselves. As soon as I looked at them, they'd look back down again. Embarrassed.

When it was time for dessert—a dirty pleasure I treasured on the outside—I turned and gestured to the boys. "Why don't you join us and have some dessert?"

"Uh, sure, but are you okay with that?" asked Nil.

"I wouldn't ask if it wasn't," I replied.

They brought their chairs over, sat down, and ordered dessert. I also ordered an espresso—another sneaky pleasure. "So, I couldn't help but notice you boys talking about us. What was so interesting? Don't any of the other parents come in to talk about what they do?"

"Well, yes they do, ma'am... I mean Claire, but there's no one else here that's like you. I mean a Convict and a Lifer at that. You're unique. I hope it's okay that I said it that way."

I didn't answer directly. "Do you know what I did to get this?" and I gestured at my brands.

"Not really, but I heard it was pretty awful and that you deserved it. Some people said you've gotten off too easy. Others say, live and let live."

"Where do you fall, Arturo?" I asked.

"Not sure."

"Well, I did a foolish and irresponsible thing when I was 21, almost six years ago, and I've been paying for it ever since. I may have caused Alejandro's father's death; we'll never know that for sure. I've taken responsibility, though, because we'll never know if it was me or someone else. It's been a tough six years. A lot has happened to me beyond these brands; they're just the tip of the iceberg. Not all has been negative, though most of it has been. I've made some truly good friends, found the man of my dreams, and been given a more than wonderful son. I'm here today because I've taken responsibility for what I did and who I am. Are you boys responsible for your behavior?" I asked.

Before they could answer, our desserts and my espresso came, and we settled back down to enjoy them. "Now, back to my question, are you boys responsible for your behavior?"

They looked at each other, unsure of what to say.

"I'm not talking in the abstract; I'm talking very specifically about how you treat me and then my son. Will you take responsibility for that?" I asked.

"Why, yes, of course, Claire."

"Good, then will you tell me what you were talking about behind our backs over at your table?"

The boys looked at each other and flushed red again.

"We were talking about you, yes. You're very hot. You know that, don't you?"

"Yes, people say that a lot usually when they want to take something from me. Let me ask you, how would you feel if we were talking about one of your moms, like she was a piece of meat to be traded or used as some men, like yourselves, saw fit," I said.

"Awful, Claire. I would probably fight them."

"Well, I can't without getting myself into deep trouble, even with you being very wrong. And I won't permit Alejandro to fight for me," I said.

"Besides, guys, she's an M.M.A. fighter. You wouldn't want to get into it with her," said Alejandro.

I smiled at Alejandro, "Thanks, Son, but that isn't my point. As I must take responsibility for what I do and have done, you boys should as well. So, I have to sit back and take it, but it's not right that I have to now and maybe for the rest of my life. What do you say?"

They looked at each other for a few seconds, and then Nil said, "I can't speak for my buddies, Claire, but I'm very sorry. I won't let this kind of thing happen again. I take responsibility for this and will make sure you're treated with respect in the future."

"Thanks, Nil, but not just me. Everyone should be treated with respect. Okay, boys?" I said.

They nodded, and I said, "Let's eat. I'm interested in seeing your school."

We walked from the restaurant to the school, the five of us. When we reached it, Alejandro said, "The headteacher, Sr. Ocaña, wants to meet you before we go to the class. I think he wants to assess if you will be an appropriate influence." He smiled, and the other boys asked if they could come too. Alejandro said, "No. We'll see you in class." I found out later that no one liked Ocaña, and they were interested in seeing how I would deal with him. They turned off in one direction, and Alejandro and I headed off in the other.

The sign over the door we entered said "Administración." Alejandro pushed his way to a long desk like you might see in a police or bus station behind which sat a battle-ax of a woman. "Mother, this is Sra. Pérez. Sra. Pérez, this is my mother, Claire McGinnis. We would like to see the headteacher."

"I'm sorry, but the headteacher is busy on a call and said that he shouldn't be interrupted." She didn't look sorry, and I could tell that we would wait a long time to see him.

"Okay, but we have a tight schedule. My mother has a prison meeting, and we have to leave to take the prison bus back. I guess we will just go on to my classes," said Alejandro.

"Wait! I see he's out of his call. I'll let him know you're here," said the battle-ax.

Alejandro smiled at me, and the two of us followed Sra. Pérez back to Mr. Ocaña's office. She knocked on the door, and a deep voice said, "Enter."

"Good afternoon, Mr. Ocaña. Alejandro Domínguez is here with the slut," said Sra. Pérez.

"This is my mother you're talking about. Treat her with respect, or I'll talk to my grandfather about the donations he makes to this cesspool. And, my name is Alejandro McGinnis. Not Domínguez anymore." Alejandro pushed past the woman.

"Thank you for defending me, Alejandro, but Sra. Pérez has the right to her opinions as I do about her," I said.

"Stop! Apologize to Ms. McGinnis, Sra. Pérez, and get out of here," said Mr. Ocaña.

Sra. Pérez simply slammed the door and walked out.

"I'm so sorry, Ms. McGinnis. She should not have said that terrible thing." I didn't move or say a thing. "Please accept my apologies. I'm glad that Alejandro brought you by today. I've wanted to meet you since you became Alejandro's guardian."

"Mother," said Alejandro.

"All right, Mother. You must admit you've given Alejandro quite an experience and a fascinating living situation. I also need to say that his grades have never been better since he moved in with you."

"I want him to be a success, Mr. Ocaña, and he never will be if he doesn't have a quality education."

"I'm proud of our school. We give the young of our best families an opportunity for a full and complete education," he said.

"Yes, you seem to do that very well. You should be proud. I want to talk to you about an opportunity, though, to stretch your students and maybe others and to give them a substantial moral grounding," I said.

"That's not our role here, Ms. McGinnis. We teach students the things they need to learn to be fair and productive citizens. It's up to the parents to give them moral grounding. I also find it interesting that someone like you should talk about moral grounding." He gestured at my chest brands. "You're doing life in prison for crimes of moral turpitude, I believe you call it. Is that correct?"

"Yes, they are, and I will tell you I had one of the finest fact-based educations one could have and was less because of it. I'm where I am today, wearing these brands for the rest of my life because I did something horribly irresponsible and protested with a typically arrogant American attitude when your country tried to discipline me. I've led a tough life because of those mistakes and want to help young people learn to be responsible members of society. Something I wish I'd known before now. I'd like kids like Alejandro to understand that behavior has consequences—stimulus and response—before they fall into the traps I did. I also think that there are opportunities for us to partner to help people like me, suffering penalties, to know that there is a life that they can have even inside the prison walls that has meaning," I said.

"That's, in part, why I'm here today," I continued. "I want to introduce a project that we're working on at the women's prison and see if there are any students, families, or faculty who might want to engage with us on it. As you know, I also am the face of the government's campaign for visitors being responsible and not violating the State's rules. It used to be on COVID-19 quarantines, but there are many rules visitors like I used to be, continue to break. The government is expanding my role to be the face of responsibility for all of us. I may never walk free again, and if I do, I will certainly not have the rights you all have. But, even with that, I do still have responsibility."

"She can't even have a phone, Mr. Ocaña. She's not used one in years. Did not know what this was," and he held up his phone. "I think there's something wrong with that, but that's not what we want to talk to my class about."

"Well, I will allow it, but I want to have strict control over what's said and how the session is conducted. I'm still skeptical of your motives, Ms. McGinnis. Among many others, I view you, personally, as a huge, ongoing danger to our community and wanted to see you thrown into the deepest, darkest hole in that prison forever. That said, I also agree with what you have said—if you truly mean it—and are not scamming us."

We spent a little more time with Mr. Ocaña talking about the script for my remarks. He said I ought to be prepared for some tough questioning from the children's parents, who he had also invited to the session. I wasn't ready for that but said that I was prepared for tough questions.

The session was to be held in a small auditorium that sat about 50 people. There was a standing-room-only crowd. I walked into the room and heard several boos and hisses from the audience. This should be fun, I thought.

"Hush, all. I'm sure many of you know who this is. Claire McGinnis is the mother of one of our students, Alejandro..." and he looked at Alejandro, who looked pointedly back at him, "McGinnis. For those of you who do not know, Ms. McGinnis was sentenced to a prison term for quarantine violation during COVID-19. Someone we had quarantined for exposure to her contracted the disease and died after several months on a ventilator. As a result, Ms. McGinnis was sentenced to life in prison, plus some years for her original offenses. Thus, she might never leave that facility alive. Except that she is here today because she has rehabilitated herself so much that the Warden of the prison, Allen Jeffer, who many of you remember as well, has made her a Trusty so that she can travel in our community in specific instances, this being one of them. She has some exciting ideas I think we all should listen to about creating stronger relationships between our city and the prison that would be mutually beneficial. I will let her speak and then for you to ask questions, but I want to encourage all of you here today to be civil to Ms. McGinnis. She comes to us at great personal risk."

I described the island reclamation project and my project for strengthening the bonds between the community and the prison, helping both the community and prisoners. Alejandro had developed a brief presentation on the project using pictures he'd shot while working there. I was impressed with the kid before this, but his abilities with a camera and the technology were impressive. I needed to ask him how to do all of this. I saw many applications for my meetings with the prison leadership.

"And so," I closed, "the ask here is for students, and maybe some of you parents and faculty, if you have the time and would like a little hard work under the sun, to come out to the Project and work with us. The product of what we do out there will help you here as much as us in keeping storms at bay and preserving our lands and wildlife. This is difficult work. Alejandro can tell you that, but it is good work."

Alejandro stepped up and said, "I've been working on the project now for the last few months. Like my Mom said, it's hard work, but working with the scientists who have helped plan this, we see the fruits of our labors. It's not just a work project but especially a science project." He looked at his science teacher, "And maybe I ought to get extra credit for it." The man grinned back at him and gave a thumbs up.

"I also want to say that this has given me a chance to see that the women in prison, in particular, the Lifers, are good people. They may have fu... screwed up, but they are trying to give back to all of us here on the Island in a back-breaking way." There was some laughter from a few of the students.

Mr. Ocaña hushed them up as he stepped back in front of the audience. "Questions for Ms. McGinnis or even, I guess, Alejandro?"

There was silence for a few minutes, and then a woman spoke up. "I won't have my child taken anywhere by that woman. I've always believed we were too easy on her, and the fact that Jeffer saw fit to promote her to a Trusty position makes me worry about the poor man's judgment. Or maybe there is more to that....."

"Mrs. Hidalgo, your behavior is not acceptable. Ms. McGinnis is here today at great peril, as I said, but that is because she believes in the project and in the value of the people she has lived with for the last six years and who she will live with for many more," said Ocaña.

Hidalgo started up again, throwing out one accusation after another about the Warden and me. I was having difficulty restraining myself and was about to speak when Alejandro spoke up.

"You all have known me for a very long time, some of you since I was born, Tia Maria," and he looked directly at Hidalgo. "I went to live with my mother to torment her, to be a daily reminder of what she did to someone, maybe—the science cannot tell us if my dad died from COVID-19 contracted from her—but found almost the same day I went to be with her she wasn't what everyone thought. She's a kind woman and deserves better than what she got, but she accepts it and takes responsibility for it. We could all learn a lot from her. I am a better and happier person because of her, even though I live in prison as well."

There was dead silence after his speech.

"May I speak, Mr. Ocaña?" asked a quiet voice from the rear of the auditorium. It was Alejandro's grandfather.

"Of course, Mr. Domínguez."

"I want you all to listen carefully to Ms. McGinnis's proposal. I plan to throw my companies' weight behind it because I believe in the importance of all of what she is doing. I'm the one responsible for her being here today. If I hadn't forced Alejandro on her, causing her significant harm in doing so, and if she had not been so graceful and accepting of my grandson, she would have been laboring in quiet at the prison. Today, she takes these risks to stand before you and ask for your support because she had no other alternative to doing that once she became Alejandro's mother. Why? Because she is a good person. Yes, as Alejandro put it, she, like many of those other Lifers, fu... screwed up, but she is paying back. Maybe soon will have paid back," he said.

"I give her my full support as I said."

The meeting went much better after Marcelo Domínguez's comments. Many people asked about coming to the island projects and working. Alejandro took names and began working on a schedule for bringing the people out. Marcelo committed to ferrying the people from the city to the islands to make things easier for everyone.

"Who was that woman? Is she actually your aunt? If yes, I've one just like her. We should get them together. Both bitches." We laughed together.

"Yes, she is. She is my dad's sister. He never liked her either, but since Grandfather gave me to you, she's been at his throat. So, I'm not surprised he spoke up, though what he said surprised me. You must have made a good impression on him. I should have warned you about her. Sorry, Mom," he said.

"I guess so, too. Here he comes with Herrera in tow. That man doesn't like me. The good news is that the feeling is mutual," I said.

"You did a wonderful job today, Claire. You even persuaded me to follow you. All I can say is that you better not be the fuck-up others think you are. I've been talking to your parents," said Marcelo.

That shook me. I thought that he'd changed his opinion about me. Clearly, he'd not. He still viewed me like dirt and checked on me.

"Here's the termination document. You'll note I added a proviso to what we talked about. If you're arrested ever again, you'll agree to leave for a place of my choosing and never return, even if that violates a parole agreement," said Marcelo.

"Grandfather, this is not what we agreed to, and I don't understand why you're an S.O.B.," Alejandro said.

"I am trying to protect my interests, Alejandro. The damages to my business caused by storms have been significant. If this woman can do anything about that, then this is an excellent investment. If she can't, then she can't. I'm willing to accept that, but if this all turns out to be some sort of con that I cannot yet figure out, then I want her to pay and pay and pay."

"Well, Grandfather, let me be very clear. The information I have about you would ensure that you spend the rest of your life where my mother is. It hides in a place where you'll never find it, look as you might. I pray, for your sake, you don't do something foolish. And if she ever must go, I go with her, understand that. You would never see me again. I would make sure of that."

His grandfather raised his hands as before, in what looked like surrender. "Sign or not, Convict. Your choice."

Herrera handed me two copies of the document and a pen. He had a smug grin on his face. I signed. They left me one and then turned and walked away, leaving me standing there with Alejandro.

"Well, that was interesting," said Alejandro. "Maybe we'll have time to travel together, Mom if you ever break the law. At least you'll never have to worry about money again. Have you ever used an A.T.M.?" he asked.

"Not in years. You'll have to give me a tutorial."

"Sure. Let's go to the bank."

The bank wouldn't issue me an A.T.M. card given my status as a prisoner, but they issued two to Alejandro, and he gave me one. Once again, I was humiliated, but it was a—microscopic—step back to everyday life.

| 9 |

The Interrogation Center

The Next Two Years:

"Well, this has been quite the day," I said on the video link to the project from the Warden's office. I explained to Lynn and the Warden what had happened at the school. With Domínguez's support, the floodgates opened, and I had twenty people, students, faculty, and parents, now signed up to come to the barrier island reclamation project. Alejandro's science teacher was excited about the project and the chance to interact with scientists working on it; he even offered students extra credit for participating in the project. Profitable for all involved.

As it turned out, the scientists were just as excited about the new participants in the project and felt that, as a result, we might move faster than planned to complete building the five planned islands. Maybe not before the next storm season, but certainly, we'd be far enough along to impact any potential storm damage positively. Marcelo Domínguez listened to this and offered more men to help to ensure that damage from any storm would be minimized a lot sooner. I was impressed at the man's civic-mindedness—way more than mine just a few years ago.

Domínguez said he would ferry the townspeople to the Camp as he had committed; his men would also bring what we needed to continue building out the islands. One barge would also be a dredger that would help us restore sands washed away in the storms from years past. Despite his mistrust and suspicion of me, he lived up to his end of the bargain. He'd told me before he left, just to tell his supervisor, when he arrived, what we needed, and he would see that they supplied it.

The first thing I said, looking at the list of the people, was that we needed food and living accommodations for the people they'd be bringing. Domínguez's men brought tents, food, and the people to prepare the food for the visitors. He didn't volunteer to feed the prisoners, and I didn't push it. All these extra hands would be worth their weight in gold for both my projects.

Almost a year passed, and the work on the islands progressed. I split my time between my work on the Warden's now many projects and Alejandro and Lynn. Notwithstanding the considerable time commitments, I also found time to continue my workouts with Paola and the other Lifers based at the prison. I lived for those times each day and the times I got into the ring to box. Alejandro tried to make these bouts as much as possible, but he was getting older and had made many friends—including a girlfriend—at school, he wanted to hang out with. As frequently as I could break away, Lynn and I went out with him. He to both be there to show us off. Tia Maria was always in the background, but eventually, she just fell off my radar.

One day after I had just beaten Paola for maybe the hundredth time, a voice from outside the ring in my corner called to me. I turned to see a man I thought I recognized. "Damn good boxing for a janitor."

That put it together for me. "It's been years since I saw you," I said. "What've you been up to?"

"A little of this, a little of that. I hear that you've been doing great things. Congratulations. I never thought you were cut out for janitor work, especially down there."

I smiled at him. "What are you doing up here? I thought you were a mole or an orc or something like that."

"One of my favorite books, by the way. We're closing shop and moving out. I always wanted to see you again, and so here I am. Come out; have a drink with me."

"Thanks, but I can't and don't drink. I'll come to talk, though. Let me take a quick shower, and I'll meet you in front of the Administration Building."

"You're not in the cells?"

"You *do* live underground. No, not for quite some time. I have an apartment on the grounds," I said.

About half an hour later, I met the man in front of the Administration building. He was sitting on the steps with a small cooler in front of him. When I came over and sat down, he opened it and pulled out a Coke. "Here, and I'm Greg. We didn't formally introduce ourselves before." He handed me the Coke and reached out to shake my hand. As he did, his jacket fell open, and I saw a large handgun in a shoulder holster. I popped up and moved away.

"I can't be anywhere near weapons. You gotta lose it if you want to talk," I said.

He got up, walked to a Jeep parked a few spaces away, and put the gun inside it. "Sorry about that... I hope you don't mind, but I talked to the Warden while you were showering. He told me about you. You've done amazing things for the prison and prisoners—even more congratulations. He also told me about your son. Is he around here somewhere? I'd like to meet him," Greg said.

"Sorry, no. He's out at the islands project with the Warden's nephew."

He smiled at me. "I heard about that, too. I'm happy for you and hope you all can make that work out somehow."

"We're working on it, and in the meantime, we're all happy with the way things are. So why are you reaching out to me?" I asked. "I don't mean to sound curt or anything, but I'd never thought we'd be sitting down just to chat."

"As I said, I was interested in what happened to you. The Warden back then made it clear that you were his property and would use the time down there as his way of getting at you. He was a prick in more than one way. We kept quiet about it because we needed the space. We don't now, and so I came to look in on you. How much more time do you have?" he asked.

I pulled the collar of my shirt over to display the Lifer brand. "I'm here for life, Greg, but I have got an agreement with the government because they used me for public service spots during COVID-19 that gets me out in another ten years. Then they deport me, and I go home, supposedly. I'm frankly not keen on that because I've got a life here now. I kind of like this place and would hate to leave it. I'll deal with that when I need to," I said.

"A little twisted in a way, but I understand."

I smiled at him. "Care to grab a bite?"

"Sure, where?"

"Two options. We can dine inside, which I'd not recommend, or you could take me into town. I need to be back by 10, though—curfew," I said.

"Let's go into town. I hate institutional food," he said. We went to the same restaurant that Alejandro and I met his friends at. We shared a large fish dish and a plateful of vegetables. Of course, there was my naughty passion, dessert, and espresso.

Greg's story was complicated. He was born and raised in Mississippi, a good old boy redneck. He joined the Army, excelled at his work, and was offered a job in interrogation. He refused initially, but after his brother, who was a New York City fireman, was killed on 9/11, he stepped up. He said it was something that he thought was an excellent response to what the terrorists did.

"Now, I know it wasn't," he said sadly. "We were told it would help us level the playing field with terrorists. I think it did, but the field it leveled was the moral one, not the informational one, and we went down to their level. We never got a hell of a lot of useful information out of our interrogations, and I lost my soul. We all did. Some of my CO's were real psychopaths. They loved hurting and killing. In any other world, they'd have been in a place like where you are. I don't think you ever belonged here, by the way. So, my hands are filthy and for nothing."

"You won't get any sympathy from me, Greg. I always thought that these programs made us worse than the people we were fighting against. I'm not a fan, necessarily, of turning the other cheek, but what you guys did was disgraceful," I said.

He blinked a couple of times and said, "Agreed. I have to live with what we did for the rest of my life."

"We're not so different there, Greg. I have to live with what I did as well," I said.

"But I guess I don't understand why you took the fall for that guy dying. There had to be a hundred ways he could have contracted the disease," he said.

"I know, but the circumstantial evidence pointed to me, and I've taken on that responsibility. I won't excuse my behavior. If I'd followed the rules, I'd be practicing law in New York right now. I didn't, so here I am, but I have an okay life, as I said. In this world, I'm as happy as I can be."

"Interesting way of looking at things... 'in this world....' Almost like a science fiction movie," he reflected.

"I guess, but there's nothing about this that's fiction."

"I hear you and am sorry that you had to experience this hell. Time to go, I think," he said, looking at his watch.

He drove me back to the prison, and I walked back into my confinement. I would have liked to spend more time with him, but I crossed the sally port at just before 10 PM. As we had driven back, we had talked more about my time between the last time he'd seen me and when he saw me at the ring. I didn't think about it at the time, but when I looked back on the evening, I saw an expert was interrogating me.

The next day was Friday, and I was packing to head out to the islands when there was a knock at my door. Greg was standing there when I opened it. He had a big smile on his face and a gun in his hand. "Back up into the apartment, Convict." He hit me in the head with the weapon when I stepped back, and I fell to the ground. As I did, I hit the coffee table, and it broke underneath me. I lost consciousness.

An unknown amount of time later, I awoke. I was hooded and tied out onto some sort of wooden frame. The room was hot, and the air was stale. I struggled a bit and then relaxed because I knew an expert had tied me out.

"Good. You're finally awake," said a voice that I didn't recognize. The hood was ripped off my head, and bright lights arranged around the room blinded me. I realized where I was: The interrogation center on one of the torture frames they called a St. Andrew's Cross. A tall, thin, bearded man was standing opposite me, smoking a cigarette. I kept my mouth shut, but when he pursed his lips, he, honestly, reminded me of a prissy fop, a dandy, in one of those old English movies where the villain had a thin mustache and overdressed for any occasion. I figured it wouldn't have been a good move to let this man know what I was thinking.

"I guess you're wondering why you're here, Ms. McGinnis. I'm Captain Caravel and have been responsible for this unit for the last ten years. The men who worked here, the man you know as Greg among them, are patriots who helped us in our fight against terrorism. When we were ordered to shut down this operation, we were also asked to tidy up to ensure no loose ends that might create a problem for our government in the future. The evening you spent with 'Greg' told me you might be just one of those loose ends. Your former Warden was also, but I believe you know he'll not be a problem for any of us. The only other wild card in this is your Guard. He was aware of this place and what we did here. He'll be dispatched here shortly."

"You present a particular problem for us, though," Caravel said. "You're a marquee convict here and an American Citizen. We talked at great length and agreed that you and your Guard would simply have to disappear. That will not happen, though, until we've explored some things with you to see if there are other potential problems with which we have to deal."

"Captain, you don't have to do this. I'll not say anything to anyone, and I know Lynn won't as well. If you need a sacrifice, then take me, not him."

He walked up to me and grabbed my face in his hands. "You're not a sacrifice, Ms. McGinnis. You're a Lifer who's reaching the end of her life, just that. When we're through with you, we'll handle you like we have with every other terrorist who we've questioned. Your body will be cremated, and then you'll be dumped in the swamp. I realize we're taking some risks with this, but you're a convict, and many people here would think what we are going to do to you is a deserved punishment."

The man smiled sadistically. "The good news for you is that you won't have to clean up the mess."

He walked over to me and put the hood back over my head. I felt a prick in my neck and passed out.

Allen and Alejandro told me about this later:

Lynn and Alejandro were sitting next to the campfire on the third project island nearing completion with Alejandro's friends. They'd spent the day working on the island-building and were feeling spent and excited by their progress. The boys jabbered among themselves, talking excitedly about their meeting with the scientists that day.

Lynn's phone rang, and he saw it was his uncle. "Good evening, Warden. How are...."

"We have got a problem, Lynn. Two guards passed Claire's apartment tonight during our normal bed check and found the front door ajar. They entered but found nothing except a broken table and Claire's gym bag sitting on the bed. We haven't been able to find her in a search of the grounds, and no one saw her leave through the front gate."

"I'm coming back, then, Warden."

"I thought you might say that, and I sent an airboat to pick you up. You're still on the island?"

"Yes, Sir."

"They'll be there in a few minutes."

When he disconnected from his uncle, Lynn looked up to see three men dressed from head to toe in black and wearing night goggles pushed up on their heads, walking toward them. All were heavily armed.

"Boys, get behind me. Quick!" he ordered. They looked around, saw the men, and then ran behind Lynn. "Get out of sight in the dunes, now."

He walked toward the men with his hands raised. "You Lynn Jeffer?" demanded one man.

"Yes, I...." and the man hit him with the butt of his gun before he could finish. He kept his weapon on all the children, prisoners, family, and guards that had gathered as the other two men dragged Lynn off into the dark. A few seconds later, they barely heard a sound-suppressed airboat taking off.

Alejandro looked up grimly and took out his phone. "Grandfather. What have you done?" Alejandro and his grandfather talked for several minutes, and then he hung up. A half an hour later, a small helicopter landed, and several heavily armed men left it. They stayed, and Alejandro got onto the aircraft and headed back toward the prison.

"Warden, this is Marcelo Domínguez. I've just had a disturbing conversation with my grandson. He told me that three men attacked their campsite on the island and took your nephew. I've dispatched some of my men to the island, but I don't think these men will be back. Alejandro is on his way to you right now, and I'd like to come as well."

"Thank you, Mr. Domínguez, but we'll have this in hand shortly. We won't need your help," said the Warden.

"I think you're wrong, Warden. Alejandro said these men moved and were equipped like they were military. You can't stand up to a military force; I can. I will be at your gates in twenty minutes, if not before, and Alejandro should land about now with three of my best men."

"Okay, but you need to know something. We found Claire has been abducted as well. Whatever this is, it involves both of them."

I was drifting along on a raft offshore from the hotel and enjoying herself in the sun, watching Hector swim nearby. Hector?

Someone slapped me awake. "Time to get up, Claire. No more rest for you."

The hood was ripped off, and the bright lights again assaulted me. Trussed out on the opposite wall was Lynn. Caravel stood in the middle of the room with three other men, one of whom I had known as Greg. Lynn glared at the four men.

"Leave her out of this. She doesn't know a thing. She was a janitor here. Just let her go," he said.

"This is so sweet," said Caravel. "She said something like that about you. Frankly, with someone like me, these are the last things you'd want to reveal. As I told Claire, we're going to question you, kill you if you survive the questioning, cremate you, and then bury you in the swamp. To give you some solace, you'll have a future together; we'll make sure that your ashes and bones are well mixed before we dump you. Your presence, in the past, here signed your death warrants. We need to know if anyone else needs to be brought in before we leave here."

"Now, this is what we're going to do. I'm going to ask one of you a question. Some answers I already know and some I don't. You won't know which is which. If you lie or cannot answer, then we'll torture your partner for a while. Understand?"

Both of us just stared at him.

"Okay. I will assume that means you understand."

He turned to his men. "Gentlemen, let's get them prepared for our festivities."

The men pulled knives from the tables and moved toward Lynn and me. When they reached us, they used the blades to cut our clothes from our bodies.

"Good. Now a little warm-up. Greg, show them the Pear and give them a brief introduction."

Greg walked over to the table and picked up a metal gadget with a pear-shaped piece of metal on one end and a key on the other. He hefted it, and it and you could hear the pieces of metal in the pear clank together.

"We call this the Pear of Anguish. We think a French robber named Capitaine Gaucherou de Palioly invented it back in the 16th century. The good Capitaine used it as a gag, but we found it works well to create many other discomforts. You put the Pear in someone's mouth or, in your case, Claire, your vagina, and then you turn the key around and around until the flanges open as far as they can go. If we pull the key out and walk away, which we've done a few times, you get a full experience of the Pear. One last thing," Caravel said, "I'm not sure the last time we cleaned this thing. Since our, uh, clients never left here alive, we weren't too careful about that. You shouldn't either."

Caravel nodded to Greg, who walked over to me and played with my sex. When it was moist enough, he shoved the Pear up inside of me. By itself, it was hugely uncomfortable, but then he turned the key. The feeling of fullness I had with it when he started was replaced by excruciating pain as tissue, muscles, and bone were shifted. I screamed.

"Stop it. Damn it," yelled Lynn.

Greg looked up and said, "Just wait a few seconds, and we'll be over to see you. When the captain says warm-up, he means that I open and close this several times, Claire. Then, I'll be over to you, Jeffer."

Greg closed the Pear, waited a few minutes, and then opened it again. This time, I just stared at the bastard. I didn't whimper, and that seemed to disturb him. He turned the key a few more times, and even though I wanted to scream again, I just glared at him. Eventually, he shrugged and turned the key back down. There was some blood on it he didn't bother to wipe off.

"This is a general-purpose torture implement, as you both will find out." He brought it up to my ass and tried to push it in. "Get my drift?" He then turned and walked over to Lynn, and he shoved it into his ass as he had shown he was going to do with me.

Caravel moved back to center stage when Greg had finished. "Now that you're both warmed up, we can have a friendly conversation, I think. My men will set you both up with the next thing you'll face if you don't answer our questions to our satisfaction."

They wrapped wires around our big toes and attached what looked like a heavy gauge wire to Lynn's penis. They shoved attached another set of cables to the Pear and pushed it up into my vagina, and opened it.

"This was a punishment that was invented by, believe it or not, a doctor, yes a doctor—had to be a real sadist, at the Tucker State Prison Farm in Arkansas. It's called the Tucker Telephone. Let me demonstrate it to you, Claire," Caravel said. One of the other men ran the wires to what looked like an old crank telephone. Caravel walked over to it and, with no more talking, turned the handle. They hit me with a massive shock, and I peed all over the ground. "You see why we had these grates built into the floor, now. I guess, though you got up close and personal with them, so you kind of know what ends up in them. The phone was developed back in the 1960s and was used until the last few years in Abu Ghraib. It was used in Viet Nam, too, but that was before my time. I'm a millennial." He smirked. I was thinking about how I might wipe that off his face.

The Warden filled me in on all of this sometime later:

He told me that Alejandro was in tears and asked, "Who would do something like this, Warden?"

"We don't know, Alejandro, but we'll find them and bring Claire and Lynn back to us," he said.

Marcelo Domínguez told them that Alejandro felt these men were part of some military unit. The one who spoke also had an American accent, he said. Their equipment was sophisticated, and the airboat was sound suppressed, so it was likely military as well. Marcelo asked if we knew of any American detachments in the area.

Allen told them that there was one but that he thought they were gone. He told him they'd been housed below the prison but entered and left it through a series of passageways that led out to the shore. They had a dock there in the jungle. They went to take a look.

The Warden and three more highly trained guards armed themselves and left in golf carts to the prison's back fence. Marcelo followed in three more carts with his men, who were all very heavily armed and, according to Marcelo, very well trained in offense. He had brought ten men with him. Alejandro fought his grandfather, but in the end, he allowed the boy to come with them if he stayed with his head of security.

When they reached the back fence, the Warden took them to a gate that looked solidly rusted shut. He produced a key, and the doors slid open smoothly, and they drove out. They went up the beach a few hundred yards, and in a thicket of jungle plants, he showed them a hidden dock. Tied to it was the airboat. Its engine was still ticking as it cooled.

"So, Lynn," said Caravel, "have you told anyone else about this place?"

He looked over at me and said, "Not a person. We were told this was a dark site. Only one guard, me, and the Warden knew about it. You supposedly shut down, though, before my uncle took over here as the Warden."

"So, you want me to believe that you never told a person about this place? Correct?"

He shook his head yes.

"Obviously a lie. You had to have told Claire. You picked her to work here," Caravel said with a sadistic smirk. "Men, open up the Pear for ten twists inside of Claire's pussy. Alternate that with three turns of the phone crank. Good ones. We don't have a tremendous amount of time. We need to blow this place up in the next few hours."

Caravel turned to the man who had nothing to do and was leaning back against the wall, "Why don't you get the ovens fired up?"

"Begin, Greg and, uh, Bill."

When they finished, I was a mess and in horrendous pain. Blood ran down my thighs. "Now, a question for you, Claire. Claire? Claire? Are you awake?" He reached into his pocket, pulled out an ampule, broke it, and passed it under my nose. I awoke with a start, moaned, and looked with unfocused eyes around the room. "There, you look like you're aware again—a question for you. A simple one, I hope. Have you told anyone here about this place? Any of your girlfriends in prison." He used finger quotes around the word "girlfriends."

I mumbled an answer.

"Did you say something? I can't hear you."

I mumbled again, and he leaned in close. Fast as a snake, I bit into his ear and wouldn't let go. The other two men were stunned, so no one moved until Caravel screamed, "Get the bitch off me!" When they pulled me off, I had a sizeable chunk of his ear in my mouth.

I smiled at him, and he glared back. Using my tongue, I caught the piece of flesh and pushed it further into my mouth, where I chewed and swallowed it. Gross, I knew, and I nearly threw up, but I was going to fight with these bastards to the end. And if I ever got my hands on Greg....

Lynn laughed out loud. "You picked the wrong tiger to fuck with Caravel. You better hope she never gets freed. I saw what she did to some pirates out in the jungle. They never found those bodies."

Greg gave Caravel a towel that he pressed against the side of his head. "We're going to treat this brief episode as you lying. Greg and, what did I call you?"

"Bill," said the other man.

"Right, sorry. Greg and Bill, why don't you treat Lynn here to a demonstration of your talents. Same as with Claire, but ream this one's ass again ten turns."

By the time they finished with Lynn, the bleeding had stopped in Caravel's ear. He looked at his two men. "Where's the other guy? He's been gone way longer than he should have. Can one of you go check on him?"

Greg left the room, and Caravel said, "We have this thing here we call riding the pyramid. It works best with women, and so we're going to give Claire a chance on it." Bill rolled a pyramid-shaped object up to me and placed it, pointing up between my legs. He then stepped several times on a hydraulic lift pedal to bring the tip of the pyramid up and into my already sore and bleeding vagina a half-inch or so.

"Now, and I bet you can feel this, Claire, there's not just a tip on this pyramid, but the edges of it are very sharp. So, not only does it spread you out, but it also slices you up. Based on what we've seen with some women terrorists who've been through here, it hurts like hell. If Lynn doesn't answer this next question, I will raise the pyramid two inches and drop you two more. I want you to think about that."

"Caravel, a question for you," I said.

"What do you put in your ears? That piece of meat tasted and smelled just like lilacs. A little feminine for a macho man like you, but kind of what I expected with how you dress and look," I said.

Bill laughed out loud, and Lynn smiled at me from his perch.

"You bitch. You'll get six inches in both directions," he screamed at her.

I smiled at him and nodded to and winked at Lynn.

"Okay, Lynn. What does your uncle know about us? We broke into his office a few days ago and removed all information about this place, but I'm afraid that might not be enough. What does he know?" asked Caravel.

"Everything," said a voice from the door. The Warden strode in. He looked at me and said, "Oh, my dear. I am so sorry," and then at Lynn, "You look like you've been through a bit, son."

"I have Uncle, but if you take me down, I'll make sure that these guys never take another breath."

He smiled at Lynn and then turned to Caravel. Before he could say anything, there was a commotion, and Alejandro slipped through the adults and ran into the room. "Mom!" and he ran to me and started to untie me.

Two of Marcelo's men rushed over to help, and two more ran over to Lynn. The Warden turned back to Caravel and said, "Captain, right? There are people here who want to spend some time with you, and I am inclined to let them have it after I see what you've done to my nephew," and he glanced back toward me, "and my niece-to-be. As an officer of the court, I also have obligations to see that you and these men, he gestured to the two semi-conscious men that Marcelo's men were holding up, are fully prosecuted. Then, you'll have time to be under my supervision here in the general population. Claire and my nephew are well-loved by prisoners and guards alike. I wouldn't want to be in your shoes for the next twenty or thirty years."

"Not going to happen, Warden," said Caravel, "Our treaty with you and contract obligates you to turn us over to the U.S. government. We'll disappear into that and be back to work in no time." He grinned at the Warden.

"Well," he said and shrugged, "there are always the ovens. Did you ever put someone into them when they were alive?"

Marcelo's men moved toward Caravel, smiling sadistically. He moved and produced a small-caliber handgun and pointed it at the Warden. "Like I said, not going to…."

A shot rang out, and blood bloomed on Caravel's chest. He looked down, surprised, and then fell to the ground. As the light left his eyes, Alejandro, still holding the pistol he had lifted from one of Marcelo's men's holsters, walked over and said, "Nobody hurts my mother and gets away with it, bastard." He shot him in the head twice.

I looked over at him and then to Lynn, shrugged, and said, "That's our boy."

They took both of us to a private hospital on the Island. It was a prominent, exclusive place and made even more controlled by many Island and American soldiers who patrolled the grounds and were housed on the floor where Lynn and I were. We stayed there for about two weeks as our wounds were treated and healed.

We heard that Greg and the other two men did end up going to jail in the U.S. Military justice sentenced each of them to twenty years in Leavenworth. Good riddance. When it came time to decide what to do about Caravel's death, everyone there said that he killed himself when he saw what was happening. The Justices said that was unfortunate and the case was closed.

We then returned to our jobs and our lives together.

| 10 |

Island Vacation After All

Two Years on Parole and Release:

Two more years passed.

The Warden saw my sentence was commuted as soon as he could after the incident. He leveraged the evidence collected in the interrogation center with both the State and the U.S. government to get their support for the release. I still had parole I needed to go through, another four years, but they said that would be under very loose supervision given where I lived and worked. While there would be a many year gap in my story, I wouldn't be completing a job application or going back to college in the U.S. or anywhere, anyway.

Part of my deal with the State and U.S. government was that I would remain where I was and that they jointly would see that I would be comfortable for the rest of my days. After all I'd been through, Marcelo finally accepted me and built me a home inside the prison walls. He told me I could come live on his estate, but I said that freedom was more than I needed and wanted. I liked the structure of the prison; I also wanted to stay near my friends. With my Trusty status over, I honestly was free for the first time in a long time. That frightened me to death.

"You cons are all the same. Once a jailbird, always a jailbird," said Marcelo. He hugged me tightly and smiled as he said it, even though there was more than a bit of truth to it—but a new love as well. It turned out that he wasn't the evil man I'd thought. He still had his problems with the Warden, but as the families grew closer, now through imminent marriage, they were warming to each other.

I continued my work at the prison and on the islands reclamation project. The Island government brought out another media crew, and they were tasked with telling the end of my story. The Warden had negotiated that even though it would potentially be embarrassing to the government and the U.S. They had agreed to that, but only if they had editorial control over the final product to minimize the consequences and prepare for damage control. The videos were well done and helped integrate me into the Island community, even though I spent almost all my time in my new home behind the prison walls, in the prison itself, or out at the project. Townspeople who came there after they saw the video were almost universally supportive. Tia Maria remained hostile, but Alejandro and Marcelo said she was the family bruja on a good day and to forget about her. Ocaña even offered me a consulting position at the school, helping grow the program I'd talked him into helping integrate the town and the prison. I took the job and have even gotten on the good side of the battle-ax.

After another year, Allen promoted me and hired me as an Assistant Warden in charge of the recidivism and rehabilitation projects, the reclamation project being one of several we implemented. These all went reasonably well. Some people, though both inside and outside, would never change, so some of the placements did not go well. But, a sign of the community opening up was that it accepted the program's failures. It probably helped that the first failure of the program came when a townsperson beat one of the prisoner placements. He's inside now, in seclusion.

I got a nice raise with that and could use that money for things for Alejandro and me. I tried to keep out of the Trust, wanting to save that for Alejandro when he turned 21. Needless to say, the promotion created quite a stir among the prison leadership team. Not the one I expected, though, when it was announced, the team had a surprise party for me and gave me gifts for this new life.

Our wedding was a small ceremony. Alejandro was proud to give away his mother to the man he also loved. In a final attempt at reconciliation, I asked my parents if they wanted to come to the wedding and if my father wanted to give me away. He told me their daughter was dead to them. I closed the door on them at that and resolved not to be bothered with any of them. I had two families here that loved me, and that was all that I needed.

After the ceremony, Lynn and I left for a honeymoon. Given restrictions on my commutation and that my citizenship was still up in the air, we couldn't leave the Island quite yet. Also, I had no passport and wouldn't have one for a little while. So, we went to the Island's tourist area, where my story started, and stayed at one of the high-end hotels, not the one I had stayed in when this all started. To add to the balance of all of this, that hotel never reopened after Desiree. Lynn and I thought it might have had something to do with how he, Paola, and I demolished the rooms.

The hotel was lovely, but I was shy about showing myself off. Between my very well-developed body and my brands and scars on scars, I felt self-conscious about using a bathing suit of any kind. Lynn said he didn't care, and he was the only one I should care about, but that didn't persuade me.

"So, no nude beach, I guess?"

"Go if you want to, but sleep with one eye open from now on," I joked back.

"How about this, we both wear tee shirts and shorts and go sunbathe, and if we get hot, that's what we wear in the water?" he asked.

"Okay...." I said a little hesitantly.

It was a lovely afternoon at the pool. We'd spent most of it lying on chaises by the poolside. I had just dozed off.

"Claire McGinnis. Is that you? You look spectacular," said a voice I thought I recognized.

I opened my eyes to a surprised Frankie Geap, the government publicist I'd not seen for many years. "Hello, Frankie. What a surprise. Not working for the government anymore?"

"Nope. I left that job years ago. I'm head of P.R. here at the hotel. May I?" She gestured at the corner of my chaise, and I nodded an invitation to sit. "I still keep in contact with some of my friends, and one of them told me what had happened to you. I'm so sorry about that. And, is this the man I've also heard so much about? I remember you from the Camp prison. You were her Guard. Our conversation at the Camp was what got me thinking about what I was doing and led me here."

I looked at her, a little puzzled. I knew Lynn had talked to her, but he had never told me what he'd said to her. It must have been good, given that this woman was as self-possessed and entitled as I was when I broke quarantine.

"Is it good to see you again," he said. "Is this a social stop? Remember what I said I'd do if you hurt, now my wife?"

Frankie looked genuinely hurt, stood up, and walked away. She came back a few minutes later and asked if she could sit again. "That was very much called for.... When you first met me, I was maybe 24 and, Claire, not that much different from you. Pretty, smart, entitled, arrogant. Lynn helped me to see that. I saw a lot of me in you as I reflected on what we put you through. You were supposed to send a message to people coming to the Island, and maybe that worked. I don't know. We certainly never had a person break quarantine again. Anyway, as I got lost in the mechanics of the communications program, I got more and more sure that 'there but for the grace of God, go I.' What I learned from what happened to you was that I could just as quickly have been in your shoes, certainly not for a quarantine violation, but for something else that I was too smart-ass about. I vowed I would change after that."

"I went back to my bosses and told them that what we were doing to you was wrong, and we ought to figure out how to deliver a message that didn't make you evil. You were being punished enough," Frankie continued. "They wouldn't listen, and so I left. Thankfully, I landed here," she said. I believed her. She was genuine.

"I can never make up to you for what we did and maybe still are doing—your billboard is still up on the way from the airport. You've become the face of what happens to lawbreakers for people thinking about doing something. It makes me sick. The good news is that no one here will ever recognize you. You've changed so much and are truly beautiful. Well, and really buff. I bet you could hold your own, right?" she said.

"Yeah, Frankie, I'm pretty accomplished in M.M.A.," I said. "You don't want to fuck with me. That's what our son says anyway."

"I hear that's for other reasons as well. I always knew that you were a fighter. I see a little curve in the nose that I don't remember being there before. You two have a son? I didn't know that," she said.

"Yes..." and I told her the story about how Alejandro became part of our family. I was starting to almost like Frankie. Reflecting on how we got here, I said, "'You can't make an omelet without breaking eggs.'"

"Robert Louis Stevenson. Gotcha. Why are you guys here?" Frankie asked.

"Our honeymoon," said Lynn.

"Oh, I'll just move on and leave you both to enjoy our place and the sun," she said.

"No, Frankie, could you stay a little more? I wanted to ask you something," I said.

"Sure, but I have a meeting I'm supposed to be at. How about we get together for a drink at, say, 5 PM, in the executive dining room?"

"Sure, but why there?" I asked.

"It'll be empty, except for us, and we can relax and enjoy ourselves." She rose, gave me a warm kiss on the cheek, and walked away.

"Well, that caught me off-guard. It surprised me to see her and for her to be so friendly to us, especially me," I said. "What do you think, Lynn?"

"Me too. But it's been over ten years. People change. Look at us," he said.

"I guess," I said as I looked at Frankie's retreating backside. "I could learn to like her, I guess."

At 5 PM, we found the executive dining room and walked in. Frankie was already there with a very distinguished-looking man and, it shocked me to see Judge Sutton.

"Hello, Claire," said Judge Sutton as she rose and came over to me. She gave me a hug and a kiss on my cheek. "You must be Lynn Jeffer. I'm very pleased to meet you, too. I've heard a lot about you." She held out her hand, and he shook it.

"Judge, I'm surprised to see you here," I said.

Sutton looked at me and smiled. She gestured to some other seats at their table, and we took them. The bartender came over and took drink orders. I still didn't drink. In part, I was unsure what legal requirements even applied around my release and in more significant part because I was afraid of what even a little alcohol might do to me after so many years.

"First, Frankie is my daughter by my first marriage," she said. "She told me she'd run into you, so we decided to crash the party. Second, I told you, Claire, years ago that I was interested in your case and would follow it. I wanted to intervene a few times, but my husband, and she gestured at the other man sitting there, told me to hold on. I realize, now, that I shouldn't have listened to him because you've suffered more than you should have for your crimes. For that, I'm very sorry. That said, Frankie said you looked terrific, and she was, as always, right. Prison was good for you, at least in that respect."

"More than that, Judge, I would never have met this man and my son if I hadn't been there," I said.

"Roads not taken, Claire, I get it, but there are some who believe that some people are destined for happiness or grief, and whatever road they take, they'll fulfill their destiny. I'm just not sure myself. I am tolerant about this sort of thing, and the reality that presents itself is what it is. In your case, it looks like the last years have left you in a great place."

"I don't disagree but wouldn't wish these last years on anyone, Judge," I said. "Another person might not have survived. I almost didn't a few times."

"Understand. Call me Alicia, please. And this is my husband, Julian Prado. You may know him as our Governor. I use my maiden name to make things, uh, less complicated for both of us," said Alicia.

"Good evening, Claire. I'm glad to meet you. Lynn, your uncle and I go back many years," said the Governor.

"Yes, Sir; he speaks very highly of you," said Lynn.

"And I feel the same way about him. I wouldn't want anyone else in a foxhole with me," said Julian.

"I'll tell him you said that," said Lynn.

"You won't need to wait to do that. He'll be coming shortly," Julian said.

Lynn and I looked at each other, confused. "Huh?" I said.

"Well, didn't you think it a little strange when you walked in," said Frankie, "that there were all these tables and no one else in here? You guys never had a proper wedding reception. So, we decided to give you one."

"Before they get here," said the Governor, "I have two little somethings for you, Claire." He handed me an official-looking package, which I opened. In it were a certificate of citizenship on the Island and a passport.

"You're now free to travel wherever you want to go. We hope you stay here, but you're truly free now Claire," he said.

The Judge handed me another envelope. In it were tickets to Venice for a four-week cruise through the Mediterranean. "For a real honeymoon," said Alicia.

I cried. "I have nowhere else that I would rather be, Alicia and Governor, but here on the Island."

The door behind them opened, and "Mom!" Aside from Alejandro, the room was packed with many people. Paola and some of my other fellow Lifers were there, allowed out to celebrate the restart of my life.

Hours later, we sat around the table with Alejandro, Allen, Julian, Alicia, Frankie, Anthony, and Marcelo. They had returned the prisoners to the prison so they wouldn't miss 10 PM lights out. I was spent, physically and emotionally. Where I was tonight, I'd never expected to be: with a loving husband, a doting son, and surrounded by people who cared for me, honestly.

I said to the group, "I wish I could say I was tipsy because I had drunk a little too much, but as you all know, I don't drink, period, anymore. I'm just overwhelmed by all of you. I've done stupid things in my life that led to other bad things that happened to others and me. I fully expect to pay for them forever in some measure, but I had an epiphany tonight."

I looked at Alejandro and said, "That means a sudden insight."

"Please, Mom, I'm not an idiot," said Alejandro.

"Sorry. I keep forgetting that." I smiled at him.

"Anyway, my epiphany: I will pay for the bad things I did for the rest of my life. They will always be here and here." I gestured to my head and heart. "But the years I've spent in prison have taught me a lot and given me things that also are in the same places. Most importantly, I've learned to accept myself and others around me with their good and bad qualities and embrace the life they've given me back. I don't know all of you well, but I love and cherish each of you. Thanks for giving me this new chance. I'll try not to disappoint you. I know I'll stumble, but I also know that there are friends around me—you—who'll pick me up when I do."

"Oh, and I'll never violate a quarantine order again."

The End

CPSIA information can be obtained
at www.ICGtesting.com
Printed in the USA
FSHW021502031221
86555FS

9 780578 303079